# Psalm 119

a novel by
**Heather McRobie**

# Psalm 119

a novel by
**Heather McRobie**

MAIA

*For Franziska*

Published in 2008 by
The Maia Press Limited
82 Forest Road
London E8 3BH
www.maiapress.com

*Psalm 119* was the winner of the first Hélène du Coudray
Undergraduate Novel Prize, supported by The Middlesex
University Writing Centre and Lady Margaret Hall, University of
Oxford, and funded by Arts Council England. The prize was set up
to honour Hélène du Coudray, who won an undergraduate novel
competition in 1927 with *Another Country* (reprinted Maia, 2003).

ISBN 978 1 904559 33 7

A CIP catalogue record for this book is available from the British Library

Printed and bound in Latvia by Dardedze Holography
on paper from sustainable managed forests

The Maia Press is supported by Arts Council England

'Do not see me only as dark,
The sun has stared at me.'
*The Song of Songs*

'Your name has been erased
from the roaring volume of speech.'
*Rumi*

# PART ONE

# ALEPH

'Blessed are the undefiled'

## LETTER

During the day:

The men here are lecherous
As the sunshine, and my legs
Are browning in shades.
The women slap my bare arms
In the market
I like it
When the UN tanks
Pass by my window
Like clouds
All dreamy and pointless.

During the day:

The city and I share sections
Of the sun with one another
Like passing segments of an orange:
    As a car-door opens
    As I comb my hair.
This is how I betrayed you
In the margins of the mornings:
Asking the creases in the curtains
    What is its secret
    Where is it weak?


I don't know where to begin:

It's always the moment when you choose to
Spread yourself into the city
Preciously, like breaking bread,
Like many suns rising from hills.
With no more need for praying then
Than artefacts need birthday-cakes,
Like a split fruit, birthing seeds:
    You open up your body's borders,
    You're your most secret state.
(It is how to die with those you hate.)


During the day:

I sent out a letter
To meet you, to warn you,

To stroke your hair homeward:
Away from walls that wait.
But it went astray. And feeling through valleys,
It woke, rebuked, the drunken spy-planes,
Shared sand with the kitchens of Jaffa.
You went astray. And it couldn't find you
Honey-kissing, your famous weakness:
Comparing the tones of the local women.


During the day:

You did not know where to find me.
You did not know where to look.
Either in the fields, or hiding from
both armies, or else lost in
The white pillars, built
between the letters, that
hold up the meaning of the word.
But because you came to me at night,
And you called me Delilah, of-the-night,
You left unread in my sent hot breath

What happened during the day.

# BETH

'Wherewithal shall a young man cleanse his way?'

It was one of the bluest and most beautiful days of autumn 2001: the sun shone and the sky dreamt of clouds, or of smoke. And walking through the old arch of her new home, Anne-Marie didn't struggle with her suitcase and hat-boxes, though blown by the fragrance of the burning end of September. She'd been forewarned that, in this country, the men wouldn't offer to help her to carry things, and her arms must have been stronger than she'd thought.

She walked up the stone steps of the college, in the dress she had bought for today. Fresh and rich-looking students struggled by or walked lightly, parents leading and in tow, depending. She smiled to some, talked briefly to a few: mainly the boys and the men. When does a child become stronger than her parents, she wondered. She leant into the Oxford-blue of the morning with her blondeness, trying to find a crack or contrast. Her decision to come here was an equation she'd figured out on the way: $\frac{1}{2}$ the quality of the letterhead and watermark of the congratulations-letter that Admissions had sent her; $\frac{3}{8}$ths the fact that, during the war, someone had touched her grandmother up at the railway station in Cambridge; $\frac{1}{4}$ the fact that her French accent would be substitute enough for any skills or charm to have friends for the first year, at the least, and $\frac{1}{8}$th her marginal preference for history books over her summer job working in a café that had an intermittent rat problem. At least she understood her reasons, at least she didn't lie, too much, to herself: this would become important as the new times dragged on and on.

She found her way up to her light room in the building's battlements. She put the hat-boxes in a row by the bed – they were empty but she hoped to fill them here. She put her suitcase full of clothes in the wardrobe, for later admiring and unpacking. The clothes were all unworn: undefiled and expensive. She shook her sweets from her pockets and they rolled about on the carpet. She tested the bed for creaks, comprehensively. She inspected the size of the expansive window without looking out at the view. Then she gazed on to the lawn, and the piles of temporary mess that were flowing from the cars on the gravelled pathways. So much stuff, so much *stuff*: she thought in her various accents, because she sometimes thought in her accents.

She watched as two large black cars passed through the arch, and stopped in the centre of the lawn. A tall woman in sunglasses stepped out and inspected the building the way a tall woman in sunglasses would more usually inspect her own fingernails for imperfections. Other members of, presumably, a family, adult and darkly clad, climbed out of their car-doors.

Marie watched as they began their unloading. Slowly, processionally, quite bored-looking, the group assembled what seemed like a large house or small street's worth of immaculate taste, of polished and scholarly curiae.

First: carved wooden chairs, three canvases of faint colour, and a desk.

Then: vases, lampshades, hard-to-carry objects, made of glass and of ceramic.

Then: bookshelves and several inviting wooden boxes, with writing on one in some kind of language. Marie was surprised, and surprised she was surprised, when she saw that the tall woman even carried these boxes herself.

Sitting on the window-sill of her new room, Marie saw a man her age amongst them all at once. He was tall like the others, but in jeans and with something written across his T-shirt that she couldn't read. He carried with one hand, and ate what looked like bread from a clear bag with the other. Marie, too blinded by sunlight to see his face, could sense him smiling from her window. It was like three different kinds of smile: like apple skin and apple centre, cheeks pushed to almost kissing his eyelashes: the two deep lines running from the nose to the corners of his mouth that made him look older, the tongue brushing upon his lip that made the grin crude and boyish. He was beautiful as a big-budget advert, and he crammed his bread into his mouth, one-handed.

Just as suddenly as they'd arrived, the dark-clothed people left in their dark cars, and Marie traced their depar-ture with her hand on the window. And the boy – or the young man: perhaps they were still in a pause of faulty labelling – stood by himself on the college lawn, looking small amongst his belongings, a rare moment for him not to be tall. He leant on a bookshelf.

'Why have you got so much stuff?' Anne-Marie called out to him in her accent. She'd come down from her room to help and laugh at him. Because this is what you do here: you go to New York, you go to Fifth Avenue; you go to university, you meet rich boys and make airless conversation, to hint at the things you could be when you're not anything yet. 'Sorry, I didn't mean . . . it's just . . .' she waved her hand at the realm of his possessions, laughing a little at how much space it took up, and picked up his football. A football. Good. So he wasn't American. She threw it to him, or at him, and he caught it.

Marie spoke English with a French accent, and French with an English one: this was a common footnote to the fact of bilinguals, she tried to explain to him, smilingly, when he asked her, but where she was from, really. Her grandmother was born in England, she explained, but had raised her in Paris, mainly through the medium of old recipes, from which Marie had learnt her favourite English word: Lard. Marie didn't know where in England half her own accent came from. 'She always just said . . . "back there",' she impersonated, pointing her thumb back over her shoulder. In the boy's family, this same sign was the universal gesture for *Europe*.

Sensing his interest, Anne-Marie offered to help him shift his colossal stuff, so she could keep talking. She took all objects regularly shaped; he carried things like lamps and crockery. The boy smiled his alpha smile straight at Anne-Marie for the first time, as she helped to carry the first crates of books up into his bedroom, which they found in the battlements facing her own.

He was called David, he told her. He knew Italian and some Portuguese, and consequently a kind of stitched-together French funny enough almost to rival her real-false voice. He'd spent a lot of his youth so far on expensive summer language courses, which sounded lonely and clean. Anne-Marie wondered whether he'd spent as much time on these programmes, and whether it could have been as lonely, as clean, as the time through her girlhood that she had spent: lying in bed, reading in bed, or holding a pillow, in bed, and dreaming that the softness was a boy like David. But obviously she didn't ask.

After her mother had walked out, into somewhere beyond history and Paris, Marie's British father took her out to Sudan, to the edge of Sudan, really the centre of the south, but still the edge; here he worked as an engineer, for an NGO, on Sudan's failing water system, on the edges of edge-towns. Marie was nine. She hated Sudan. The towns were nowhere, mentioned in no books she'd read or wanted to – and Paris, she knew, was an ultimate somewhere, which other people dreamt of, in second-rate dreams. She forced her father to send her back to Paris, where her paternal grandmother looked after their old house: she did this by herself, refusing food for days and eating only sweets in secret, then chopping all her blonde hair off, then moving all the house's possessions out on to the bare front lawn during the night.

Marie never thought about the look on her father's face that last day, in the heat and her razed head burning. When it came to her briefly, she thought about important words and places. Because she never lost the imaginative colonialism of a nine-year-old: the world, for her, comprised of centres and peripheries, pulsed outwards to the edges, like jellyfish, and she would only deign to live in the middle of it, to be or at least touch the nucleus – only the centres had offerings for her, the centres of cities, the centres of facts. She vaguely dreamt of noun-based heavens, where she'd inhabit the core of a golden word – Chanel or Stendhal, Oxford or War – any word as long as it was coveted and magnetic. Her father would still send her letters, but to her these were brown and nothing, the opposite of gold.

'Will you go back one day?' David asked, neutral, not looking at her. He was mostly hidden by a lampshade that he was trying to fit through the door.

'I'd rather go to hell.' She said this because having an accent meant you could say things like that to English boys. 'So where did you grow up?'

'You know, just London.' He frowned as he manoeuvred the lampshade around the curve of the stairs.

He described his home and family to her like performing a card-trick, deftly, confidently, averting her attention away from the crucial issues with minor sparkling facts, while Marie was stumbling over with a coat-stand or Marie was nearly putting her foot through the back of his guitar. The two made a pulley out of a blue bed-sheet to bring a painting up into his bedroom. The Cohens were academics, art critics, curators, general moths around art – he listed their names to her for nothing – but still they'd manage to produce this David, a little trunk full of their looted treasures, which he seemed about to empty here and become light. He either didn't notice or mind when Marie dropped his antiques down the stairs.

And then when they'd housed all David's junk and treasure once more under a roof together, he made Marie coffee and got out 'one of my top three favourite' (was he joking?) sets of coffee cups. They each sat on a box of books and finished eating the bread that David had shoved into his low-slung pockets. The two looked around the large, white room, and at each other.

'It's a lovely view,' she said.

'The whole reason I chose this college.'

'Not because Oscar Wilde went here?'

'What's that supposed to mean?'

'Nothing. Nothing. It's just, you have very – good hair.'

He laughed with the right side of his mouth and leaned sideways. 'You're not a very nice person, are you?'

'Can I steal this?' She pointed to the rich coffee cup as she set it down on the floor. It was at least top-three in the list of stupidly pretty objects she had ever seen. David smiled again and finished his drink.

'Only if you take care of it.'

'Really? I was only joking.'

He made a smaller smile and looked at her when he talked now. 'My family thought Oxford's things might not be good enough, so I should take some of ours just in case.'

She told him, almost without thinking, that she came by train, by herself, with only her clothes and her hat boxes, that her rich clothes were only a hoax to trick the people she thought she'd be meeting here. She told him that, really, she didn't have anything: only her grandmother, rich in old biscuit-tins and drawers of saved, snapped, birthday candles. Then she smiled and she said: 'I knew I'd accidentally tell someone about it right away.'

So they agreed to rid him of most of what he had, if

Marie could prove she could find good use for it.

But not for nothing: he made her choose between his candles and bronze paperweights.

When she picked the coffee cups over the printed family stationery, it was immediately clear to them both that she had made the wrong choice. But too late.

Pointing with her eyes closed she lost the bedsheets to the bookends.

The plates were won one by one through the naming of notable literary anti-Semites.

He asked how much she was willing to give for his lovely Georgian chest of drawers.

And she let him have his little victories, and accepted his rule not to take what she did not understand: he could keep his chess set, his Hebrew books, his telescope. Then they went through his heavy, heavy boxes of books, Marie pulling them out pile by pile, and reading the backs of the ones she didn't know. She brought him up-to-date on the latest gossip on the Western classics – 'you're not allowed to like him any more', 'shit', 'colonialist', 'shit', 'merde', 'pederast' – until the mountain of thrown books grew around her, which was a strange way of unpacking.

When at last she stopped to pick them up, David explained to her why he had so much stuff. This was a fraction of the junk of his house, and his house was an extension of a famous museum, where his father was the director. Where Anne-Marie had broken candles, he'd had Canalettos; they'd filled a silent house in the same way.

'Can I have the keys to it?'

'What?'

'To the museum.'

'Well. Um, I don't think there are *one* set of keys, I think that . . .'

'What are in the private rooms?'

'Mainly things no one wants to see.'

She thought about this. 'No. That's not true. There must be things that people want to see but can't.'

'Why?' He said. He did that smile thing again.

'Because why else wouldn't you give me the key?' She decided not to be fazed by his beauty and looked him in the eye.

'Well. OK. I've heard that there's a room of Victorian sex toys.'

'Are they any good?'

'If you get a tetanus shot first.'

It took the two of them seven trips to carry her new possessions to her room. By the end there was no one left on the grass, and it had started to smell of the evening. He carried the last objects over the lawn for her – an atlas and some oil-paints – and, as he set down the last of Marie's winnings for her, he said goodbye to her in her doorway.

# RUMI

In the beginning, there were just caves. He sat in his and I sat in mine. We read our books: they were the same book, the same script, the same language of evenings, our alphabets curling up upon themselves the same way, vowel-less. As lovers spend their nights without consonants, so the praying man spends his without vowels. We ran our fingers over the words, to sing them, or to shout them.

The man in his cave, and I in mine, watched over Afghanistan, like devils and angels, angel-devils, devil-angels. The world was watched over now by the devil-angels of untried men: in those camps they weren't guilty or innocent yet, they were like a sun and moon in the sky together – you have to remember, right and wrong were suspended in these times, easily as a paper-law. So there can be no judgement in the story here, born as it was in this pause of certainty. It has to be an offering to no one.

We were all working busily on our useless offerings. The man in his cave, and I in mine, sent our little ones out into the world – mine pointless love poetry, his four blazing planes. I watched as the sky turned the colour of wine, as in my poems, and I did not realise for a long time that it was the colour of blood.

It hadn't always been like this. I sat in this cave for eight hundred years, and at one time – can you believe it? – there was too much love between people on earth. I would write a few lines of verse to God:

> *If you can't smell the fragrance*
> *Don't come into the garden of Love.*
> *If you're unwilling to undress*
> *Don't enter the stream of Truth.*

and everyone would say – what a beautiful love poem, Rumi. Who is this woman? How did it end between you two? I'd try to ignore their responses, and I would write again to God:

> *I lay in the dust at your feet,*
> *My heart entangled in the curls of your hair.*
> *I've had enough. Bring closer*
> *Your lips and let your kiss release my soul.*

and again, people would say to my face – you're a sly one, Rumi. Who can this woman be?

Is there anything more useless than love poetry? Eventually I stopped showing them what I wrote: I sloped off to my Afghan cave, for peace, for God, and for love of him.

Centuries passed: easily during the day, and slowly in the night. Breeze by breeze, my cave became a library of scrolls: they blew in from east and west, instinctively seeking out the dryness, as though old scrolls and old caves dreamt of each other. The Torah, the times of Jesus, love poems in every language, curled up like cats to lie together next to my works and the Book. Sometimes, in the night, I thought they had sat there so long that they had started to melt into one another, but during the day I'd think: Rumi, don't be crazy, cut back on your wine.

Then the man moved into the cave opposite me, and I forgot about my parchment. He became my book to read, when I felt too unwashed to pick up the book. I watched him closely, my strange brother, my opposite – we were as the same hand, once as an out-stretched palm, and once again as a fist. I could feel him watching me. And after he sent four burning planes into the great face of his enemy, more bombs came to rain upon the holy dust of my cave.

It was a hard decision, to leave. I was born in Afghanistan, in Balkh in its shy glory, home of Zoroaster, dreamer of pale reds. And the caves of the mountains had made themselves warm as wives for me, since I'd retreated here from the world. Heavily I packed the scrolls I could carry, gravely selecting the first, then blindly grasping the rest, because it was too painful, having to choose: like choosing between children, I thought. I rolled them into one another, that they might learn each others' contents. The man in the cave opposite watched me crawl out with my scraps of belongings, scraps of my scrappy limbs. But he pretended to be blind to me, as he pretended deafness to the love we'd read nightly, from the same book.

I'd done this before, this scrambling, and that all made it worse somehow. When the Mongols came, or when we smelt them coming, in burning breezes not so different from these, my father drew the family close round him, and we walked towards the west. All through the whole universe that Khorasan was then, we walked in endless slumber, nudged by the western breeze of Nishapur or roused by smelling-salts of the strong poems that blew from the residue of the Ghaznavids' old courts. And all the way to the glassy blue of the Turcomans - only then they let me stop, in Konya. Imagine walking from Afghanistan to Turkey and it's less surprising that I spent eight hundred years in my cave recovering.

Later they called me Rumi - the Roman, the European. And I liked being The European, but I didn't like that they'd forgotten how far we'd all walked. My bones remembered, talked about it all my nights in the cave: remember Rumi, that time of grinding bones, remember Rumi, the aching, the hard floors. I was made by walking, it was my backbone. My mind belonged to my feet, my spine a great long line of our slow-moving caravans. I made my first poems to have a place to hide in, a home away from walking and walking. And this time, I knew, I read it in the red sky, the walk would be further, and it would feel longer. I could feel people marching to the east as I was marching to the west: little swollen Rumis, sick-looking Europeans, stinking of words, ideas all swarming them, like so many malarial flies. It was a time of prayerless, pointless pilgrimage, a mockery of pilgrimage. I don't know what star they thought was leading them: the sky was too red, the night I set out, to see any stars at all.

The roads down from the cave were a different kind of hard to that which I'd grown used to, all those hard years ago. My legs chastised my weight, as my eyes chastised the sun. I walked for three days from the mountains to the mountain-edges, where the edge of people began. I passed women fleeing, in every direction, wearing the colours of the night. I passed men in uniform, who caught the women, and ripped the night from their skin. The roads became the colour of scrolls, and many dusty sandals wrote on them the stories of war, only to be written over, with other stories, other cries. I grew thirsty and asked for water. My tongue had grown incomprehensible, as it had slowly consumed itself inside its cave, inside my cave. The men pushed me aside, busy writing their panic in the pathways. Old man, I could see them thinking, how have you survived so long when my young boys have all been snatched from me?

I came to Kabul in the night. My mouth was aching like an old dancer. The sky would feed me only red and black. There were great fires, there were great beasts in the heavens, and there was a great cry of women, women and women and women, as they all at once fell to the floor burning: their robes turning traitors against them, aflame and eating the flesh. There wasn't a house in the city that could shelter me now: tiny limbs lay before their doors, to ward off wandering poets; cries came out from within the walls, to ward off words that would describe.

There was so much fire that it seemed to obliterate the scales to measure the fire. The clocks were ablaze. The mosques were ablaze. The prayers that flew up from the mosques flew up, ablaze, and burnt their pleas in the sky, but the cries for mercy were sent back down to the city, where they burnt the rooftops of the oldest houses. I could not enter a mosque to pray: dead bodies and rocks were guarding every entrance. I made my way towards the library.

The library was still awaiting the fire, its contents trying to moisten themselves with the stories they held inside. But their pages had long since cracked, like chapped lips, shrunken in drought, and drained of beauty. I didn't recognise a single book.

I found a table and unrolled my scrolls. I had visions that they had been burnt in the fire of the city, that the flames could sniff out either their dryness or their preciousness. I went through them one by one, as if counting the heads of my family.

In between the pages of a long psalm I'd long ago copied out – the longest psalm in the book – was a letter in a language I hadn't seen for centuries. Not since my late life in the Turkish lands, a land woven in mixed languages, years before my departure from the world and to my cave. The characters on the scroll bristled back to life, shocked at the new air, prickling to have eyes upon them again, and they lazily stretched out all their meanings, like limbs after a sleep. The letter wasn't addressed to me and I felt God watching me reading the contents. A man trying to tell a woman he loves her. A man trying to tell a woman that he's sorry. This was no business of mine. And yet the name, and yet the language, box-shaped, thick, Semitic characters, packaging gifts set all before me, or else shaped like baskets holding snakes. The letter was signed Shimson – Samson – 'to use'. But what use was it to me?

Then the night came on. The pages in the library, all their flesh and freshness long gone, bared their teeth at the coming fire: only such words of hate could have baited the burning rain to come. The fire answered their defiance, the roof melted above me like snow, and the fire took up its throne in the library: the walls and I all bowed and buckled before it. I ran out of the burning building as though I had spent my eight hundred years in dreams of running. I ran as though I was writing new poems with my feet, as though I wanted to blaze R-u-m-i across the burning land. For many miles and many days and far away from the city I ran, chanting words of love to God to keep me running.

After much wandering, much closeness to blood, I found a new cave and I opened up my scrolls again. The fire still hadn't found them. And all at once I was touched by something. It had been so long, so long, that even my dreams had forgotten it. I was touched by a woman, a beautiful woman, a woman's words. Delilah's writings burned on the pages, as though I held Kabul itself in my hands.

# GIMEL
'Deal bountifully with thy servant'

Marie was the one who took first, then, and David the first
wronged, and the richest – no richer than the other boys
here, but to her: singled out. They began their intertwined
life regardless, and soon it would be hard to weigh the debt
or trace the first tossed stone.

They fell in love and it was simple, like a fact to be learnt,
because it was as though they lived in a world that wouldn't
allow prefaces or lengthy introductions any more. Love had
to be the start of the story, gotten over with quickly. And
people couldn't fall in love at length here – nothing could
happen here, slowly, under stark lights: conversations about
war, terrorism, conversations about love – that didn't sound
like mockery or like a Footlights sketch. Even the people
who did really fall in love here knew that, even the people
here who were dragged into real wars and real terror knew
that – and Marie seemed to almost love the fact itself.

So they watched each others' borders closely, and kissed for the first time in the college library. She saw David spend the week building up to their kiss, watching her lips bubble up and back down again, like the islands of Hawaii on a geological atlas, as her level of understanding and interest, at every introductory lecture, waxed, waned, went out. He told her her clothes were unlike anything, and her sentences all unintentionally funny, like she lacked a natural voice. Perhaps she had no inner monologue. Perhaps they had let her in by mistake. Everyone always thought that about themselves there, she knew; she was the only one that it was really thought about.

He seemed to love the fact she had no fixed name. She'd answer to Anne-Marie, Marie, Maria, Marianne and even Annie; he wondered aloud how much further he could stretch this. Marie was happy to deal upon the lazy assumptions sort-of English men had about sort-of French girls: that perhaps that when she sighed in bed the sounds would escape, wrapped up, not these punctuation marks: ' ', but these: « », and that many things might be brought to them through these soft and agile implications.

And Marie – Maria, Marianne, Annie – for her part, felt funny and flustered and happy and anxious and cross and queasy whenever he smiled at her, and whenever he didn't, which left little time to do anything else in those first Oxford weeks. In her mind his surname, C-o-h-e-n, had been written out somewhere in the lettering of Chanel, and she could really think of no higher compliment. She wanted it written on every bottle in her bathroom; she wanted it stitched on the small silk labels on the inside of her clothes.

The kisses happened, for the first time, when they were trying to study for their first essay. They'd left their work too late, and sat in the library at three in the morning, which they'd learnt was the only place in the city that stayed open all night. They were reading about the end of British colonialism: Marie pulled out a volume of the Cambridge History of Empire and watched as the two volumes next to it fell out and on to David's feet. Ssshes fluttered by from the nearby library desks because David shouted something out in the dead room.

She came up from picking up the books. He put his left hand under her head, and his right around her waist. She dropped the books again and he kissed her again. They picked them up again, and kissed, dropped them again. He left her room at seven o'clock in the morning. 'I just remembered,' he whispered into her ear, softly so it tickled, 'that I have to write my essay. See you tonight.'

And so it was that David hardly ever saw his own room after that, now that Marie's contained not only all his finest possessions, but also Marie's warm body in bed. David was the one sent out to the place on Little Clarendon Street that stayed open late, to bring back the three meals they had forgotten to eat while kissing and arguing and taking Marie's dress half off and putting it half back on again, needlessly, and giggling. One of the arguments was that she should wear dresses with fewer buttons at the back.

And the first few weeks between them were a freshness of feeling, light despite their daily, laughing, fights, amongst the stale, familiar sights and words of their new home. They'd lazily read in the park and he'd fall asleep with his face in a book, or fall lazily again back into bed, and then he'd fall asleep with his head between her legs and Marie would rub his back if he woke up in an angle that hurt. Some nights they'd bring wine up into the battlements, or she'd sacrifice her expensive shoes to nights of climbing the walls of Botanical Gardens, as he'd sacrifice observing the Sabbath for the heavy work of sleeping next to her. They lay on their backs in the nearby fields even in winter, and tried to teach each other their languages. She lent him books and they ate her sweets, the ones that appeared like miraculous springs and visions from her pockets, like she was Bernadette.

David dressed as if he was poor: jeans and vintage store-bought T-shirts of old protests ('Free Nelson Mandela!', said one; others hid, under fadedness, badly drawn cartoons about recycling). Marie was poor and dressed as if she was rich, fine linings and logos crowning her like tributes. Perhaps she'd realised it earlier than most girls: women aren't let off the hook of their looks just by choosing not to cultivate them. Or perhaps the mindlessness of her hair-dresser-trips, her French copy of *Vogue*, the aligned perfume bottles in the bathroom that they shared now, were like the mindlessness of prayers by some Persian poet: the abrogation of the mind before beauty. It could as easily be prayer, and not pride, in what they liked to dream of as the start of the new Biblical times.

She tried to explain some of this to David at one of their early outdoor Hebrew lessons. It was as if she wanted to speak a language with only one letter – alpha – that the whole world should consist only of that letter, and everything else was washed up, defiled, in the world of motorway signs and lost car-keys, caca and pipi, other libraries – a world where messages were sent with letter-heads less embossed than Oxford's; the world she had come from and wanted, with him, to escape.

*

The one thing that Marie had was her grandmother, and she died before Anne-Marie could introduce her to David. A phone call came about her death from a hospital in the suburbs. The letters that followed addressed to Marie were the French condolences of debt.

David didn't complain even once when she worked her way through several of his 'top-ten-favourite' (was he joking?) T-shirts, destroying them with more cried-out mascara than could have painted the Turin shroud. She didn't talk to him about her sadness, only asked to borrow enough money for a new, designer, thin-pleated, knee-length, satin black dress.

And she put the dress on gently over her black underwear, a kind of seduction in reverse, and just as slow. David left his history book unread to clasp the hooks she couldn't reach; the book lay open at a point near a warning. Marie's hair kept getting in his way, and she held it up, in front of a mirror, as he knelt to fasten the satin as close to her skin as only he had been.

They left straight away for the funeral, the longest they'd stayed dressed since the kiss. They came to Paris by the Eurostar, ready in their black clothes. They skipped quickly past the French security guards, because Anne-Marie had dropped her ticket in the toilet, or else had used it to blot her shiny new lipstick. But even in those early months of the new fears, France didn't seem to worry about the terrorists; the guards looked the kind of bored that said: go on, I dare you. Marie wondered for a while, the secret 2001 thought, of where she would have hidden her bomb, if she'd had one.

The funeral had been arranged mainly by Marie herself from across the Channel. It was as alpha as she could have hoped. The two of them quietly played the usual guessing game for people in a room of French men a certain shade of grey. *Collaborateur* – *Résistant* – *Conspirateur* – *68 rioter*, their eyes went through the icy room, dividing weak heads into lines for his own purposes. It was good practice for their arithmetic: calculate how old an eighty year old-looking man would have been in any year of the last century, and what kind and what weight of weapon he would have carried accordingly.

And Anne-Marie looked at the statue of the Virgin, while the French men spoke of their respects. As the sun was not shining, all in her honour, the statue's skin colour on the hands and head looked slightly off-tone under the window, and the face had the beautiful, dented, lazy-plasticine cheekbones of a young Kate Moss.

*

David looked over as Anne-Marie was contemplating all of this perfection. He told her later: it was then he decided to love her. He went through her flaws in turn, when he'd finished mentally marching the men into two carriages. The vanity, the upturn of her nose, the small mole on her breast that he'd found, the unshakable imperfection of her accent in whatever she wanted to say: they all walked the same gang-plank under his orders. He too had been unsure, it seemed, almost until watching her put on her funeral dress, whether he was going to love her for real or only pretending. Like a young man in love in happy times, he wondered what he'd ever be able to give her, then remembered his money, and her sweet, holy superficiality. And he kissed her on the steps of the church, as shy as though he'd never seen her naked.

And David was keen to put his trust into Marie's love, and her new-found and near-enough orphanhood, and then put his trust somewhere in his mind, similar to the mental furnaces that he'd built at the funeral. He told her the pin number for his credit card on the train back from Paris, writing it out using one finger and his other palm as unmarked paper. She seemed to understand, and said she loved him too.

# ד

## DALETH
'My soul cleaveth unto dust'

And to feign a level of responsibility for her glorious blaze of spending, which continued back in Oxford like the banner of a crusade, Marie got a job in a bookshop, against the university's rules. She'd sit there and stare at soft, slouchy English girls, in their boyfriend's cricket jumpers or their French Connection dresses, with their hands in their pockets, or free time on their hands. Their hair shifted from blonde to brown and back again like flick-books, they were a blur of the things in the world that weren't her. They made her feel like her limbs were too long, like she had a pebble stuck under her tongue. They made her spend a semester of book-scanning wondering what it would be like to be a boy, and on the end of their beauty. Like a Daddy-long-legs, she thought. This was her favourite English word after Lard.

And then she'd come home and lie on the bed, in her own or David's still over-full room. She'd read out articles from a fashion magazine, in a voice that suited the flat, perfumed crispness of the printed page. This was perhaps what she resembled most of all: something blank whose words you'd have to imagine being spoken realistically.

David was reading his history books of the week at his desk with the tall brass candlesticks. Marie began to happily plait and unplait her hair, using the window as her mirror. Suddenly she sat up, remembering. 'Shit.' Her accent was strong today as perfume: it sounded more like 'sheet'. 'I forgot to buy a new dress for that meal at the new professor's house. Oh shit. Shit.'

'We'll buy one at the weekend then.'

'But the professor's meal's tomorrow. Sheet.'

The professor was going to teach them next term. They read that he was the son of an Egyptian politician, and had come to the teaching of Middle Eastern politics after an early career lecturing in literature. He'd made the headlines the previous year, when he resigned his post at Yale, and cited Islamophobia among the staff. He had a long face that suited the papers; features the equivalent of large font – easy to read. David Googled his name and read everything he could about him, until Marie had fallen asleep, one half of her hair left unbraided.

The dress Anne-Marie wore to the meal at the new professor's house was ivory, with grey and silver stitching on the shoulders, and wasn't worth the money that one of them had spent on it. The sequined stitching itched so much that David had to wrap his hands around a cool wide glass of white wine, then rub his icy palms across her neck.

The two arrived late: they'd fallen asleep and then lost their way to the great white house in Jericho. A man in his fifties answered the oak door, holding a bottle of wine, with a tea-towel over his shoulder, and asked them to come in. The professor explained that he had to finish off in the kitchen, but 'by all means have a drink or two while you're waiting, guys.' His accent was not English and not anything else. Marie noticed this as David dragged her over to the alcohol.

Ten or eleven other students were already there, at the table set for food, or else were sitting, in secretive twos, and talking, on the professor's wide old staircase. Anne-Marie had met a few of them, in her trips to the library to distract David from his study and to drop books. She vaguely remembered names for them like Heather, Poppy, Daisy: names that were nobody's favourite flowers. She'd seen them shaking their heads when Marie had yawned all the way through lectures, rustling and nestling in woollen English shyness, and she prayed that all the threads of all their sweaters would snag. She went up to the bathroom and put cold water on her scratched shoulders. She took off her dress and laughed to find herself in her underwear in a professor's house. She didn't use the mirror to watch herself, but the reflecting surfaces of framed photographs of old, Egyptian women, her mouth hovering over their hairline, or her living eyes floating on their dead cheeks; overlapping femininities.

\*

During the meal the professor had cooked, David watched out for signs that anyone else lived in the house with him. He didn't have a wedding ring on his long, balanced hands.

41

David realised, embarrassed, that he didn't know whether Muslim men wore wedding rings. The professor saw him looking at his hands and smiled at him.

Food and wine and conversation passed around: Italian food, French wine, talk of war-time. The professor listened smilingly to everyone's excuses for poor test marks, late essays, and the various wine stains on carpets. He leaned in to people without them noticing the shrinking distance between them; he listened to people without them noticing all the deft tricks of his listening. And so it always felt to the other person that it should be his turn for talking – and when encouraged to speak he would rise to it as though accepting a delightfully unexpected gift.

He shared photographs from his recent travels, while evidence of his earlier journeys were thinly framed upon the walls. He spoke softly of the unfolding war in Afghanistan. He'd witnessed the opening weeks of the conflict, on a one-off correspondent trip for a Canadian magazine. He spoke in primary colours – red poppy fields and blue-scarved women – not the language of dust and fire. Every nineteen- and twenty-year-old was asked their opinion on the war: maybe it was wrong of him to teach them that anyone's view on a war would matter now, but still they formed an emergency cabinet around the dinner table.

The professor took no special interest in Anne-Marie, even as he could see down the top of her dress when he walked around filling up wine-glasses, to the part where her light French suntan kissed her pinkish English pale. At the long, wooden table, on which she'd been given an awkward chair, Marie fidgeted through the three courses, and whenever she heard the phrase 'the thing about Afghanistan is . . .' she'd put her hand down the top of David's trousers under the table, her hands cold with wine, then hot with drunkenness – until one of the snappy, short English girls noticed and she thought that she should stop.

\*

Other evenings followed in the house in Jericho – war mixed with wine mixed with laughter – and David would find some way to be alone with the professor. And from the lamp-lit corner with the old globe, in one of the Georgian front rooms, David learnt both the principles of Muslim marriage and the fact that the professor was divorced. This gave him only the slightest head-start over the other students when it came to their essays. Since they'd started writing essays for the professor, there was so much to be sorted out, and quickly – from poverty-gaps to violence against women, from rentier economies to identity politics – so much that couldn't be solved or advanced, without hearing what a boy called Oliver from Haberdashers had made of the current developments in Syria. They all had their favourite Arab revolutionaries.

David didn't realise he changed when he was around the professor, until one evening at the house when he noticed that Marie had gone back to their college without having said goodbye or dragging him off with her. When he came to her bedroom later that night, he wanted to say sorry for something – but instead somehow felt that he had to share with her: 'The professor said I could be the best student he's ever had.'

'David, I'm too tired for you.' It was the only time she'd ever say that.

At the last meals of the term that the professor hosted,

David left Anne-Marie to fraternise with the lop-sided, soft-eyed English girls, unwrappable in their woollen layers of shyness. He and the professor took up their corner, and he listened to more tales of photogenic liberation armies. They sat at the dining table when talk had tired them, and David was given a potted history of the land of Palestine, with thick glass salt and pepper shakers standing in as shifting borders over time. Sometimes he wanted to break the glass shakers and mix the two into sand, but then felt stupid, like a boy, for thinking that.

He'd go to visit the house during the day, too, explaining to Anne-Marie that the professor had offered to give him Arabic lessons. Some nights he would return very late, smelling of a mix of two wines, mumbling as he undressed them both, or pawing her out of sleep.

*

Marie found herself often alone for her first time since she'd met David. Even his possessions bored her when she was by herself, after the first evening of trying on regimental jackets which David had taken from the museum's store-rooms. She went to work more often. She even put some effort into her studies. Still most of her note-taking stopped mid-sentence, like the deliberate mistakes in Arabic tapestries. Like most girls and many women, Anne-Marie's mind was as graphic as it was squeamish of bad taste, and she spent her time at her table in the bookshop either mentally undoing David's belt, or else avoiding the gaze of girls her age, who swayed as they stood at the shop's book-cases, tilting like long grass to try to read the book-spines.

She didn't begin by avoiding their gaze. But the wash of girls that drifted past Marie's half-hidden face – her burning face, that felt sore and needed scratching, that she pulled her Dior cardigan up to cover when she had nothing to do with her hands – seemed all to be in her own reflection – parading all the colours that her hair could be, with eyes and breasts in turn smaller and larger that averaged out to her image. She couldn't watch them and she couldn't stop. She couldn't tell if it was attraction or disgust: the bitterly chaste side of the feeling she got when walking in Pigalle or on catching a glimpse of the kind of pornography intended only for men. She couldn't stomach it, but her mind was clamped open, like a kind of mental dentistry. The girls were all untouchable – not the way they were to men – more like the way that your spleen is.

And so she would feel sea-sick all the way home, as she could not shake their blend of shifting images. They danced around in her head as eternally as Kate Moss in that music video: their faces turning into her own and back, as Marie reached out for them in her soft, drunk nightmares. She spent more nights in her bed, alone, as she realised that, in some way, David was betraying her now, and dreaming only of himself: she knew she did not understand an affair with an idea. But then she too was only ever really looking at herself. She bit her lip as the English girls, their hearts in their pockets, their legs only hinted at, perused her wares and slouched heartlessly towards Jericho.

*Dear Delilah,*

*I brought down the two towers that held up the temple, an arm round each, like a staggering drunk, but sobering under the coolness of marble. I stood like a child between towering parents, then tugged like a lover undoing your belt. The columns had the polished feel of your thighs, and I pushed in between them the way that I'd done, to settle for sleep, that final time.*

*And it was as though I'd pressed myself into the gap between two Hebrew letters – deep into the murmuring calm of unmarked vowels. And, for the first time, blinded by the strangers who'd enslaved me, I only felt the whiteness of things, and I was as peaceful as sleep. Dying wasn't so much of a climax for me as a happy snore.*

*And I don't know how people felt as they walked into the gas-chambers. I'm not saying I do. I'm not saying anyone can. But perhaps it was the same sensation that I had then: of rising above the particulars. That, along with all the things that were being destroyed there – the lives and the objects and the words – so all the instruments once used to gauge destruction were also being extinguished: crushed by that which was unthinkable; the incomparable than obliterates scale.*

I'm not saying I understand. I'm blindly feeling the idea of it. From what I understand of it, from what has filtered down to me: when there were pogroms and state-sponsored ghettos, the Jews who were living through it – Jews not so very different from us – could only speak in a flood of Biblical images, searching for something alpha enough to stand for the scale of their loss.

But then, once they were in the death camps, there were suddenly no metaphors; there couldn't be, when nothing happened there that could be referenced to mere outside fact. And I think that it was with the same crushing pain that I stitched myself into the books that day: the gasping feeling that I was, right now, living in the paradigm.

And I know that you don't understand why I am writing yet.

And I don't want to make it any easier.

If you want to try at all, it won't be easy – and let's neither of us even dream about succeeding yet. I'm writing – that's a start, I think. Just to study the distances that we'd both have to travel across, if we ever wanted to meet each other again.

I don't know whether you saw me that day.

I listened out for your voice in the temple.

They dragged me out to dance for them, lined up their women for me. A Philistine boy held on to the rope around my neck, and I danced my tortuous way to the centre of the temple, pounding my feet into the floor and ignoring the pawing of the thousands. The Philistines tired before me, just like they'd done in battles. And as they began to pull away, all panting with their exercise, I asked the boy to take my hands and let me stroke the pillars. Those were the words that I used, stroke the pillars, stroke them: tender as dancing. I could feel the young Philistine boy shaking as he took my ripped palms and placed them on to the columns.

And it was this boy, as docile as honey, and not you, that was to be my last contact with the varieties of the living. I've often wondered, as I wondered then, perhaps you were watching, and perhaps for you, at least, I was to be the last imprint of the world's sensations. Where among their number were you? What were you wearing, as the roof came down? I know that you like it when men make a note of these kinds of details. How far in that moment was the space between your body and mine? And were you turned towards me or away?

I didn't make the classic error of thinking G-d was on my side. So amateur of my later suicide-brothers: to think He has a stake in it. I had had enough of His game with me, of being the chosen puppet for him, like every Nazarite led by a star, his cock, a commandment: this way Samson, that way Samson, lead the people, slay the lion. I had long been seasick with the tugs of these fatalities. I admit that when you cut my hair I felt a kind of relief.

The rope that the young boy held around me that day was like a joke for old time's sake, made of a farce of twine where it had once been His ever-vigilant loving, dragging me through the world. That day I was already severed as normal human children, leaving normal human wombs. Or so I imagine: like a practice Jesus, I was one once cruelly implanted into the unsuspecting womb of a barren woman, on a hot a day in the sand. I was a stranger to myself and to my family since the time before my birth: as strange to those who saw me G-d-like as I felt strange before G-d.

And in the temple, at the centre of everything, I only asked to die as I had lived: yes, like this, as a stranger to myself. It seemed like the closest I could be to my own experience: I would not have anyone else's. I refused to be touched by any vision of His. And so, as though a bug in amber, it would be my strange home forever, the friendly pillars rushed to capture my eternally confused face. The one last thing I asked of Him was: let my soul die with the Philistines.

Let my soul die, crush my immortality. It says something of

how tired I was. It does not saying anything of how tired I still am. I had been so bound up by

G-d, so sore and slammed with fate: only this could be my release. It was to be my most beautiful mistake.

So perhaps you know now why I'm writing.

I can't help you with this, Delilah. I can't lead the way to an understanding. Either you follow me or you don't. But I hope you understand what I'm asking of you. Perhaps we can carry each other.

It's hard to be a myth to yourself, Delilah. But then I suppose that you know this already, that it's learnt in the closeted perfuming hours, where women are training themselves into being mysterious. It must be hard to be mysterious to yourself. Yes, I suppose that you know this already. I don't suppose we really taught each other anything new.

I can't be preserved as a stranger to myself.

And I need someone else to restore me back to who I really am.

Being lost unto yourself, being frozen as an alien entity – it might have let me study more fully all the contours of my own condition. And I suppose I always knew that it was going to bring me no comfort – that's why I asked Him for it – let my soul die, lick no wounds of mine, I want to extinguish myself with this familiar bitterness. My soul cleaveth unto dust, as one of the psalms said that was not David's.

And yet bitterness quenches nothing at all, and dying a stranger is not the peace that I thought it would be. It is not a thing like sleep. It is like having no eyelids.

And yet, with your hands on me, I might rest, with someone's love I might remember my centre, the part that's not just the lacking of G-d. Still, I know that there are many deserts and valleys of aching forgetting between us: we both revoked our permission to be dreamt about in private, and exploded ourselves into a myth or a Biblical silence. That is a hard terrain to know where one could start to look.

Why do we need another body lying next to us, to bring us back to ourselves? Why do we hand over all our own log books into the unsafe hands of another soul? And how can severed people even tell the story of trying to get themselves back? I thought that if I sent you this, Delilah, you could help me look for where to start beginning. But maybe even this is too hopeful: the wishful thinking of those without wishes or dreams.

The only things that a myth can listen to are the stories that have vanished from the world. And this is how I have passed my time, in the library where I sit and write this letter, to my lost and darling Delilah.

And among the songs that have been laid at my hard and flinching feet, my feet that callous with every note of beauty, were the almost-silent Etruscan psalms that reached me from the sea. Or else they are songs that have crept through those pillars of white on our pages which hold up the meanings of words. The Etruscans who had ferried so many of their alphabets.

It is a prayer for them and it's a prayer about them, about the source of the raining of glory that their people worshipped with their souls. It is a song about money, and that's why I think you'll like it. I'm allowed to make these kinds of jokes. It was brought here to me here in the library where we're sustained by a lack of evidence. It is beautiful to me because there are no supporting documents. And I wish I could sing the psalm stroking your sleeping-head, like I used to, because all the lines in it are for both of us. I have dreamt about it for more years than you have locks of hair:

It's said that they were strong
*And quiet as poisonous wallpaper,*
All as good and as heavy as gold
*In nights as cold as silver*

Stoking the Jesuit ocean
*They levered the skirts and the sails*
And oh how rare the collisions were
*And how well-worn the trails*

*They were a seafaring people*
*Their heavy work was love*
*They carried rocks and messages*
*They traded with the Gods*

And though their songs were old as sex
*They were stitched to no future tongue*
They brought her statue by helicopter
*They made his out of bones*

*They were a seafaring people*
*Although they lost their way*
*All laden with their promises*
*They washed up in the bay*

Their treasures are beached on other shores
*His crucifix hits a girl's chest*
My eyelids are heavy as jewels now
*Her gold band has come back to rest*

*They were a seafaring people*
*Their heavy work was love*
*They carried rocks and messages*
*They traded with the Gods*

And you may meet them under glass
*Or drying out on earth*
Those who we sent into the world
*To do our dirty work*

*They were a seafaring people*
*Although they lost their way*
*All laden with their promises*
*They washed up in the bay*

*So that is why I am writing, Delilah. I need you to give me myself back.*

# HE
'Incline my heart unto thy testimonies'

David's lessons with the professor continued. He walked through Jericho, a bottle of wine wrapped up in tissue paper, and quietly practicing his vowel sounds. Anne-Marie stayed in, watching *The O.C* on David's computer, or staring at her mounting work through the new mascara she was trying, that sometimes bound her eyes blind, but looked beautiful.

And so it was that the more time David would spend learning Arabic, the more spending took place in Marie's endless time – entire afternoons of praying to the logos and prices at perfume counters, like rows of holy votive candles, or at displayed lipsticks lined in rows of red, like uniformed Napoleonic soldiers – and the more warm seats in Oxford coffee-shops were taken up by Marie's itchy thoughts, Marie's stockings and their constant need to be adjusted, while Marie's thoughtless hands clutched vaguely at lakes of hot drinks.

Perhaps on a good day she'd bring an unopened book. More usually she'd put her empty hands inside her coat, or occasionally see if she could get away with stealing a saucer as she walked out of a quiet restaurant. At the end of each day she'd proudly present to David completed crosswords from the *New York Times* and the *Guardian*. She tried to subscribe to *Pravda* to see if they did crosswords in Russian, and what kind of clues they would have if they did. To reward this sort of hard work she would settle down to re-reading Françoise Sagan, because to her it was the 1950s name for *The O.C.*

David would return from the professor's house with presents of red wine and red stories of the Lebanon, blazing like a crashed plane, as he tried to navigate his way between his upbringing and the teachings the professor had given him on Israel. But Anne-Marie would soothe him then with holy coolness of her shallowness, and they would fall asleep in their peace.

And then, just before the start of the war that was to shadow them, the professor introduced them to Mohammad. It happened at one of the professor's parties, the photos of past wars looming. Mohammad studied law, and went to one of the newer colleges. He was their age and almost as tall as David. He'd grown up close to David's house in North London; they didn't recognise each other. His hooded looks from under heavy eyelids meant you had to lean in close to him, and the quietness of his deep voice meant you had to lean in closer. Mohammad had met the professor at the Amnesty International lectures that were held in Oxford every year, and he'd been invited along to one of the now-regular dinners for the students taking the paper in Middle Eastern politics. Marie got talking to him, standing on a landing, waiting for the bathroom, to apply her mascara again – as she had vowed to herself to do every time she heard the phrase, that evening, 'the thing about Iraq is . . .'

And it came to pass that at the end of the evening, as two of the entirely knitted English girls helped the professor to carry empty plates to the kitchen awaiting cleaning, and as Marie was giving up on bathrooms and telling David to apply her mascara for her, sitting at the corner of the long table, fighting each other harmlessly for more space, Mohammad walked up to the two of them and said: 'It was very nice to meet you.'

'You didn't.'

'I'm sorry.'

'You didn't.'

'I'm sorry.'

David laughed. 'I mean, you didn't meet me.' He stood up. 'I'm sure that it would have been very nice, though, if you did.'

'Oh. Right. Yes. I'm sorry.'

Marie put away her make-up bag, and stood up next to David.

'Your name's Mohammad, isn't it?'

'Yes.'

'Do you want to come with us to get some ice-cream?'

At G & Ds ice-cream café, they had a book at the front where customers could petition for new flavours of ice-cream to be made up, and they let you stay there on one coffee until they closed at 1am. So every satchel-carrying student was camped out there with a pad of fluorescent Post-It notes, half-working and half-thinking up a flavour of ice-cream worse than the current favourite – 'Friday Night

Sundae' – Stella Artois-flavoured sorbet with kebab chunks blended in. David and Marie spent so long arguing, pushing each other's borders for more air, more space, more rightness, on the walk from the professor's house, in the ice-cream queue, and at the pastel-painted tables in G & Ds, that Mohammad stood there long enough to read the entire list of potential, horrific desserts.

\*

And then it was that Marie was lying on the bed in her room, books around her like attentive children to a governess, and David sat on the chair he had given her, putting the markings of vowel-accents over his Arabic exercise. They were going for coffee with Mohammad later that day.

'I don't like his name, it's too long.'

'It's the third most popular name in Britain.'

'It's not a good name for a friend, I mean, it's too formal. Like you couldn't whisper it in his ear.'

'Don't whisper in his ear then.'

'You know what I mean.'

He came over, she stroked the hair that had grown longer, and the books that had grown on their bed entered again the market-place of the mess: waiting shoes, yawning coffee-cups, potentialities of paper, and the snake-skins of the dresses she'd shed. And so they arrived to coffee a little late, because David wouldn't let go of her wrists so that she might brush her hair, and he undid the buttons of her coat as quickly as she could do them back up again. Mohammad smiled so open and kindly when they came in to the café that they both felt sorry for having made him wait.

Anne-Marie was happy to have found a quiet friend, who wouldn't always be in her ears like David was, like the roaring of the sea. They'd walk through the streets, Mohammad listening to her laughing complaints against everything, Marie trying out different kinds of high-heeled walk as she pretended to care about politics. She decided to teach him how to dress, he taught her some Arabic to rival David's, together they flirted with the idea of learning Farsi ('it'll be more important after Iraq'). But usually he was silent.

David was perhaps more in need of him than Marie, not being as used to living in the pockets only of one finely lined person, and the two boys would go to lectures by international-relations professors, then run back down the aching streets. David wanted Mohammad to take him to the Middle East, and to come up with arguments to use on his parents – who saw a strange, late teenage rebellion in their son's sudden interest in Islam. But Mohammad would look even more uncomfortable than when Marie adjusted her stockings in front of him, as he tried to explain that it was really none of his business.

ו

# VAU

'Take not the word of truth utterly out of my mouth'

One day the following term, the professor came to Marie's bookshop, as she sat gazing at sideways, smudgy girls in English dresses and opaque tights.

At first Marie was going to pretend that she didn't recognise him. He was probably just shopping, for a bit of light reading on misplaced polarities in post-colonial literature, for his day off, for fun. And he could get her in trouble for having a job during term-time. But he came closer to where she sat, and was unbuttoning his navy coat, as the shop was heated for the English winter (and the autumn; and the spring). Had he seen her? She hid behind a large print book, ingenious disguise. She'd heard that Oxford was the place where MI5 recruited its spies. She heard him coughing and looked up.

'Hello.'
'Hello.'
'Hello.'

She couldn't very well say the fourth hello. She drummed her pencil on the desk, distractedly.

'How are you?' he said.

'I'm well. How are you? How was Lebanon?'

'Very well.'

'David said that your photographs were wonderful.'

'Yes, well . . .'

He was nervous, it seemed, to be around her, like he was making an effort to enjoy her. They spoke about the books on the counter that she leant on. He had rolled up the sleeves of the white shirt he wore. She remembered the professor had begun to teach David Arabic, and asked to have her first lesson now, if he wasn't too busy. She said it because it was something to say. He took it as a gift. He took a pencil out of his pocket, and went through the first letters of the alphabet with her.

He leaned over her to correct her malformed characters. 'This must be like a child's handwriting to you,' she said.

'No. It's a mixture of a child's and an adult's. Adults make different mistakes from people learning for the first time. Like, see here, how small you've made that noon letter.'

Just as he was going to show her how to put diacritics on to the words she'd written in her half-child handwriting, she realised she should have closed the shop up an hour ago. The professor stood around, with his heavy navy coat back on, rubbing the back of his greying head, to answer her questions about dialects, sometimes having to shout so she could hear him back in the stock-room.

He helped her to pull down the metal grate that covered the closed shop's windows. 'How do you do it when you're on your own?'

'Oh, I always find someone to help me.'

The professor frowned a little.

'Well, thank you for the Arabic lesson.'

'Would you like to get some dinner?' he asked her as she was walking away. She turned around and looked at him properly. His eyelashes cast small shadows on his dark and ageing skin, and this made her say yes to him. And so it was that he took her to a little French restaurant on North Parade, a quiet Oxford street probably sponsored by Americans to maintain its unlikely English charm. Streamers zigzagged across the tiny buildings, which were painted a different colour each, like it was done up for the 1953 coronation. Marie didn't know what to do with the visual alphaness of the city's exteriors, so decided it was all rigged for her, like a film set.

All of the waiters knew the professor. He was hugged by an older, fatter, more worn-looking man, who stood near the door in a crumpled suit. Holding the menu with a little apprehension, she decided the thing to do was to be the one to suggest that they got a bottle of wine. He said it was an excellent idea, in his own accent of not-anywhere.

During the meal he showed her the photograph in the corner of the restaurant of Diana Mitford kissing a pig.

'That's obscene.'

'It happened right here.'

Marie decided not to believe it. It was probably a still from a film.

He showed her the restaurant's fireplace that had been there for five hundred years. She asked how he knew all this and he told her that, when he first came to Oxford as an undergraduate, this was the only place in the city that would serve him food with the other students, instead of at a separate table. She was not sure if she believed this either, it seemed so far away.

On the way out he showed her the room where a future American president had seduced the daughter of the Vice-Chancellor. Walking back to his house, he detoured to show her the alpine-like pond where, he told her, girls from Somerville used to sleep together in the moonlight as part of some sort of Greek cult. Through a blur of wine, in the front room of his house, he showed her a photograph he had taken for *National Geographic*, of Afghan soldiers on horseback. Through a blur of toothy-grinning, drunk and failing at straight-facedness, he showed her how a scar on his upper arm turned into a smile when he tensed it. And then it was that through a blur of wine, upstairs, he showed her that not all men make love like David did, like they are jumping into the sea. Because this is what you did here. You go to Egypt, you see the Pyramids; you go to university, you sleep with professors – you choose to fall in love with the wrong things – and give yourself, with embarrassing ease, to any unsuitable, worn-out person or idea – poetry or socialism or men who still held doors open for women – it was just so much sight-seeing.

\*

And so it was that, the following morning, they discussed what to do about what happened, but didn't get very far: their conversations were never to have conversational endings, felt forever like a series of unclosed parentheses they'd have to go back and finish off another day. As Anne-Marie was turning to leave, the professor opened the door for her and they kissed again until the latch clicked itself shut. His kisses were like flicking through all the pages of a paperback book: the noise of slight rain on rooftops. Marie did no work that day, or the next. The professor left the bedroom twice, once for his lecture, the other time to open the door and tell David he would have to postpone the Arabic lesson. Marie said nothing when he came back up to tell her this.

The sheets on the professor's bed were the colour of wine, and Anne-Marie kept them around her as she began another Arabic lesson. The professor sat on the edge of the bed in a shirt with thin navy lines. Marie looked serious, did not even play with her hair, and pushed away the new-found kisses he offered, when she was wrestling with a question or a verb. She asked him whether Arabic was like music notation: the way the vowels are written in, like marks upon a clef. He didn't know, and was more interested then in discovering the small mark upon her breast, but she liked this train of thought, and tried to pursue it as he tried equally hard to distract her. She practised saying her alphabet musically, as the professor kissed her stomach. She was suddenly full of questions about language, because she'd always suffered under her own funny tongue, because she was still shopping for her perfect-fit voice. Can you be born into the wrong language, the way that transsexuals feel born into the wrong body? What would they do to fix you?

Still politics slithered into every private corner, every sanctuary, into the professor's bedroom: if you averaged out one hundred sample conversations in Oxford, England, late 2002, your sum would be a rough sketch of their exchanges – especially when Marie made the mistake of bringing a newspaper with her when she knocked on his door in the evening.

'The war on terror is racist. The war on terror is a fraud. And they can't even say it's a well-intentioned mistake. *They know what they're doing.*' She heard all this reverberating through his chest, where her head would lie as she practised her Arabic. 'It's a war to kick the world into agreement with America.' Marie agreed, obviously, so did every single person she'd met: this was 2002, this was a place where talking about things was a job. It didn't seem controversial enough to have caused problems for him at Yale, or insightful enough to get him a professorship at Oxford. She happily assumed he was talking without subtleties for her sake.

'OK. But what can we do about it?'

'That's not really the way to think about it. Saying it's wrong *is* what we can do about it. We can't be held responsible that our so-called leaders are a bunch of arseholes . . .' He said arseholes not assholes. British colonialism won out over American imperialism in his voice.

'Fine, well, I've said it. If you say there's no more I can do . . .'

'That's not what I mean.'

It wasn't that she disagreed. She agreed completely, because he was the one who'd been paid to teach her: our thinking is still colonialist. She agreed: our liberty is a sham. She agreed: he told her Edward Said had long since shown the fabric of our thinking as couture lined with the silk of dominance, still beautiful, but unwearable. Of course she knew that every venture before her had been a great and violent dead-end: it all gave her more confidence somehow.

'OK. So what do we do now?'

'Well, it's not really that simple . . .'

'Maybe not for you, but – OK, for me, for people like me, my age, what do I do to make sure I'm not being colonial?'

'That's not really how to think about it, as, sort of, not being caught.'

'But what I mean is – if I don't want to reinforce, perpetrate, the cultural imperialism – what do I do? Edward Said and you, you do all this talking and talking, but you know, you never answer: *what now*.'

He stroked her hair indulgently. 'You don't need to do anything, my love.'

Sweet Maria, born without colonial sin.

These conversations played themselves out without too much personal interest from either of them: they were just so many rehearsed steps to be gone through between kisses. The professor seemed to admire her lack of interest in politics and the democracy of her offensiveness. He gave her one of his mother's old headscarves and she stitched it into a slouching dress. He gave her a kafiya from his student days and she turned it into a mini-skirt.

And when they tired of talking about wars he'd teach her more Arabic, although learning Classical and modern Egyptian dialects together was like baking a cake every day and then trying to undo it every evening. For a long time she'd only learn the initial position of the letters of the Arabic script. When David saw her practice sheets in their bedroom, he told her: 'You won't be able to read anything like that. Except maybe neon signs in Dubai, or something.'

'Fine. That's all I want to know Arabic for. For shopping trips.'

'Suit yourself.' David returned to his translation, and

Marie sat in front of the mirror brushing her hair like she was getting a sin out, snapping some of the ends and pulling faces at herself when she did. The two of them nestled into their own silences, and he didn't watch her like he'd begun to: the night before, he'd seen her on the steps of the professor's house at midnight. She said he wouldn't have seen her unless he was going to the house at that time too.

\*

Anne-Marie adjusted her dress under her light peach coat, while standing on the doorstep of the professor's house, during the day this time. She hated the first ninety seconds of his company, the sinewy, quiet awkwardnesses that had never completely left their entrances: taking off her coat, choosing somewhere to sit, or else waiting for him to kiss her, or fix her a drink that would lick things smooth for them both once again. She wondered how few the awkward seconds would become before she'd be able to love him. But today he was wearing a shirt rolled at the sleeves, opened at the neck, which narrowed the awkwardness to just under a minute.

Later, she lay on his iron bed as he went through the notes of his morning lecture. 'It's strange to think how much of my time I spent reading the Qur'an to practise my Arabic. For someone who doesn't believe it, I mean.'

'It is strange in many ways,' the professor replied, without looking up.

'But I worry', she said, overdoing her accent, 'what if it suddenly goes out of fashion? I think of all those clothes I never wear now, which I thought were going to be timeless.' She sat up and continued, mostly talking to herself. 'And just think how many men in Oxford can speak Russian needlessly, because of the last century? It's not like we can get our money back, if we don't need the knowledge any more . . .'

'Well, I think Islam's here for the long haul, my love.'

'Like little black dresses.'

He put his papers away and came to sit by her.

'It's important that you learn it. Try to apply yourself to something other than yourself.'

She kissed the top of his head. There was only the sign of a hint of a future baldness. She tapped her lips with her hand the way she did when she was thinking about something, or else trying to look like she was.

'But, think about how strange it is. I'm not even twenty and the thing I do in the daytime is learn a language whose alphabet goes the other way from mine. I just . . . think none of us ever imagined that faith would come and bite us on the arse like this.'

The professor shrugged his shoulders. 'I suspected that it might.'

'Don't lie.'

'But I did. I'd foreseen it a few times.'

'No one could have. Except God or something.'

'Everyone always thinks that they live in Biblical times.'

Anne-Marie rolled her eyes at him, the way she had to, because he was too much older to always be arguing with. While he talked at her about war and language, she'd lie on the bed, full of questions she really wanted to ask him: how much had underwear changed in the time in which the professor had been sleeping with women? Had he seen trends, of bras and of underwear lines, come back and forth, like hemlines, in cold, small bedrooms in New

Haven, and through the long-ago nights in Cairo? What was it like, to have loved women, over the decades when women had changed so much, if they had really changed so much? Had the clasps gotten easier to undo, from a practical point of view, with the alleged rise in promiscuity that occurred before she was born? She asked him about this last one.

'There was no rise in permissiveness, it was a lie.'

She'd heard so many commonly known things described as lies by him that she was a little unsure of this.

'Except in England, of course,' he continued. 'But that was not in the sixties, that was during the war, when all the colonising American GIs were occupying and spreading syphilis. In fact, the "V" in "VD" originally stood for "Victory".'

His anti-American sentiments would break out at times like this, like an embarrassment, a hiccup, made as they were for a more obvious, less arch era. Most of all, Marie was embarrassed to hear the professor describe the United Nations as 'the new tool for beating up people who aren't white'. As an eighteen-year-old, she knew of course that the Americans had sponsored the Taliban, but the professor's list of all the other things they'd secretly orchestrated grew too long to be of interest, and didn't fit so neatly with the fact that he also called them all lazy. He was, she thought, too intelligent to carry off his little conspiracy theories, what she called his old-man rants, which in Marie's mind were only held by ugly people who made their own internet sites and couldn't spell. His crude anti-Americanism was the spit that spoiled the wine of his mind's subtleties. Still, she liked the look on his face when he said 'America', a face like violence, and desire. The creases of his mouth drew down. His eyes would become darker.

And it was during times like this that she'd realise that he wasn't just older but old. With her head on his chest and looking southward, she knew that her experience with the professor was alpha partly because this was to be her first encounter with the unlovely flesh that was the house of humanity's greater averages. She learnt that there were creases that weren't designed to be kissed. There could be grey hair everywhere there was hair. And from under the slight overhang of his uneven stomach, his penis became a kind of after-thought. He was handsome but he was old now: his handsomeness trying to pretend he was only on holiday here, in this age, and could come back to thirty or forty when it liked. As she thought these thoughts he stroked her hair as if he had all the time in the world. She shifted her head from his chest to the bottom of his stomach.

'What does it feel like, being fifty-nine?'

'Very good.'

From where her cheek was she could feel him smiling, with his eyes closed or else dreamily flickering.

'When I'm fifty-nine . . .'

'Hmm.'

'what are the chances . . .'

'Hmm.'

'that a nineteen-year-old boy will want to come to me . . .'

'Hmm.'

'and want to kiss my stomach?'

The professor made a contented noise from somewhere deep in his throat. And when he spoke it sounded like he was trying to talk without parting his lips. 'That's not really fair, Marie,' she heard indistinctly through the rumble of his chest. She sat up.

'Why not?'

He smiled blearily, drew her back down towards him, and spent some time kissing her hands. 'Do you think that when I was nineteen years old I could have had a girl like you?'

'I think you probably could, if you worked hard enough at it.'

'But there weren't any girls like you when I was nineteen years old.'

He settled himself for sleep, but Marie sprang up again like a mechanical doll, and covered her warm body with the sheet. Sadly the moonlight rested determinedly not on her body but his. 'You can't say you're owed this now just because you didn't have it then,' she said, into the darkness, in her voice for teachers. 'All those centuries and centuries of sex without AIDS, just imagine' – she closed her eyes to imagine – 'no fumbling for condoms, and no midnight conversations about all of your medical details. All those centuries, centuries and centuries . . . you didn't exactly make the most of it.'

'Who, everyone or me personally?'

It was clear that he was in an inexcusably good mood.

And the nights in his room seemed to pass in and out through the windows they left open, in a lightness that remained no matter how often the professor would try to talk with heavy anger, or Marie would try from time to time to rattle them. They were frivolously happy in a peaceful country, despite all their best efforts to the contrary.

# ZAIN

'Thy statutes have been my songs in the house of my pilgrimage'

And before she knew it, the term was drawing to an end. Contentedness had made her sleepy: because her hair had been stroked by the professor and her boyfriend too much, and put her mind at ease, and because doing nothing was now her job, so it tired her like a work-day. And so it was that she started to spend the days and evenings neither at the professor's house nor in David's bed, but instead too sleepy even to get up and eat more than a few of the boiled sweets that were forever being born out of her bags and pockets.

She'd lie in her bed every evening, alone and stroking her own hair absent-mindedly. And she would nearly be asleep. She would so almost be asleep. But she was awake, not in her head – this part of her was at the best of times as alert as an episode of *The* O.C.; the flimsiest of Françoise Sagan novels – she would be thinking, achingly alert, somewhere in her intestines.

She'd shift around in the crisp pyjamas David had bought her, feeling an awareness of something there, not hunger, for an hour or two, of a question, or an itch, of a keenness which was dull. Until, suddenly, began the sharp, careful needle-point of pain, shuddering like a caught automatic drill, genius in specificity as doctorates on sonnets, thundering down one side of her stomach. She'd have to curl up and bite the corner of the duvet. She hugged the pillow for comfort the way she had through her eighteen years in France.

At first she thought it was appendicitis. She called a doctor and was laughed at. She lay on her bed too shocked to cry and thought of words she seemed to associate with old colonial wars, like 'ruptured spleen', like 'flesh wound'. She had to stroke her stomach, over and over – not sensually, like a lover, or like a pregnant woman, but more like she was trying to make a snake out of plasticine. But she couldn't make anything, and she couldn't make it stop.

Eventually she tried eating. It took a long time for it to occur to her that she'd forgotten to eat anything that wasn't artificial, and this might not be a good thing. So she found a piece of bread in the communal kitchen, and they eyed each other on the table. She thought about the English word Yeast. She vomited water up into the sink. And this, she discovered, was to be the tragedy of Anne-Marie's precious stomach: the hunger's intensity lowered no standards of what she could or would eat. She didn't know when she'd ever been so critical of what she would put in her mouth.

She lay sobbing, crying for herself, on her floor until the morning, then slumberingly staggered out to Waitrose supermarket. Then she slept all day, slept all through when the shops were open. And she awoke in the night again, her shelves bereft of food, feeling half-dead and aching all over, but worthy only of the most quality stuffed vine-leaves. By the fourth day the homeless men who sat outside Waitrose began to recognise her as their own, as she stared down the sliding doors at 7.57, 7.58, 7.59 in the morning. This happened maybe three or four more times: Marie would lie in bed all un-hungry and sleepy and genuinely believing that this time would be an easy ride, her eyelids even gluing themselves shut slowly and prematurely, until about two o'clock in the morning, when the night pangs started again. And after an hour of shifting unhappily and praying vaguely to nothing, she'd decide she couldn't fight it alone, and had to run through the ancient streets: sniffing out anything she could.

But Marie, for all her blondeness, was not completely useless. She'd attempted to stock up her own kitchen shelves like a proper person would. She set her alarm for Daytime, despite her sleepless nights of hunger, and would go down to the supermarket, faithful as a church's flock, fuzzy-eyed and meekly clutching the thin metal handle of a basket. She cupped the avocados shyly to measure their inside-colour, selected her favourite bowls of olives, and adorned herself with armfuls of expensive organic cereal boxes. And, just then, always and like clockwork, she would begin to reverse each detail of her movements, putting each contemplated foodstuff back in its place, slowly, like flowers to a grave, and walking out of the shop, backwards, like she was at the Wailing Wall.

'I just feel disgusted at everything,' she'd try to explain to David when he came round to find her curled up and clutching her soft stomach, or biting at her pillow in pain, but still refusing to let her holy insides touch anything as dirty as food. 'I'm hungry but I'm too *disgusted* to eat.' She liked the English word Disgust because it had a gloss of morality, but what she really meant was that the whole world was: gross, or yucky, caca and pipi, the smell of the stuff, all of the stuff, it just made her want to vomit. And then she did, in her long white dress, and into the sink in the kitchen she'd never cooked in.

So supermarkets were out of the question, and cooking too ridiculous. After a week even seeing the marketed food made her retch in the shining aisles. She had to rely on her clandestine networks of culinary support. At three or four or five in the morning, after she had had enough of any-minute-now-ing for hours wrapped in her bedding, sobbing only for herself, she started to get up and go round to the rooms of the people in her college that she'd vaguely got to know – at least those who'd made the mistake of seeming reliable to one who is ravenous.

And so she began to be the sweet, soft-voiced acquaintance who had to ask a favour, very sorry, just this once. After that she began to be the friend whose charming acts of eccentricity were, just now, beginning to show. And then she became the funny story to tell to another friend, laughing, charmingly. At some point after that she became a joke. The four-in-the-morning fool, drunk-looking but much less fun, who occasionally brought her own bowl when she dragged you from your bleary fat girlfriend, clung to your old bed-smelling T-shirt and sobbed to you the words: Greek yoghurt.

A very beautiful moment would be when a nice English girl would bumble out of her room in her dressing-gown, hand Marie her bread or cereal, and Marie's response would be: 'Yuck. Don't you have anything better?' But they couldn't have understood: at times like this she would have strangled someone for a fix of the finest pesto and sun-dried tomatoes. It is not rare to want to kill for purity.

It was Mohammad who saved her from this potential life of gastro-crime. He was on her list of people to call on for a fix, but lived ten minutes away, in a college whose new buildings looked like giant typewriters in the dark. But one night after term had finished, and all the English girls had slouched home with their boxes of slippers, kettles and extension-cords, Marie climbed the wall to get to Mohammad. Or just to get her hands on any food that her stomach would sanction.

He answered the knock on his door quickly, and Anne-Marie was surprised that he didn't look surprised. Perhaps David had told her about her sleeping patterns. Did David talk to Mohammad about her? Her boyfriend hadn't been around very much himself, in the last weeks of term: there were always more Arabic classes to go to. Marie explained about her hunger and her sickness. Mohammad looked mild and sleepy when he was just default-Mohammad, so when he was feeling mild and sleepy he looked like a Disney cartoon of a lamb.

'Maybe you're feeling bad about something,' he suggested, barely parting his lips, mildly, sleepily.

The word Guilt was as unexpected to Anne-Marie as an outbreak of smallpox in the twenty-first century. But she thought sleepily about the professor. She thought, counting hazily, how much of David's money she'd spent. She thought greedily about hummus and delicatessen pitta breads and pesto and well-displayed bowls of expensive tapas.

'Maybe you're right.'

'Do you want to talk about it?'

'No. I want to eat.'

And so Mohammad led her to the kitchen that he shared with four physicist boys who liked to stick informative charts on their communal walls. He poured her a bowl of cereal, his eyes almost too nearly closed to see what he was doing. He found some bananas in someone else's cupboards, and left a note – of course Mohammad would leave a note – to say that he'd replace them. He found some bread and jam and cheeses. They carried it all back up to his room, Marie deftly grabbing a box of someone else's biscuits that were sitting by the door. Then he seemed to watch her through his struggling eyes, for the next twenty minutes, as she munched away at the assembled offerings, and he picked up her plates when she was finished. He poured her a glass of water. They sat together on his tidy single bed.

'I hope you're feeling better.'

'Those biscuits were heaven.'

'Marie, do you want to talk about it?'

'I don't know what I want.'

'Neither do I.'

Was he about to kiss her? She ran through a quick list of necessary components. It was a Thursday morning: nothing special. They'd been eating cheese and bread: nothing special. They were listening to an album that they both quite liked, I guess, but then again: nothing special. And her hair wasn't neat but nor was it dishevelled. Was he leaning towards her?

'Have you seen the news?' she said suddenly, the way that someone else, but not her, would say 'that's a lovely dress' at a party.

'Yeah, I've got it as my homepage. And I've been down-loading special reports on the World Service.'

'Oh, right. Can you show me how to do that?'

'Yeah, of course.'

'Actually, Mohammad, could you just do it for me?'

'Yes, of course.'

'Well. Thanks for the food.'

She decided to go straight to the professor's house before sleep washed away Mohammad's mark on her, and now that she had food-energy. She left the college full of something new, and Oxford gently gathered her into its morning mist. A film crew was coaxing the dawn up with their imitation offering of lighting-bars and bright white sheets, and the sandstone buildings looked on impassively, as though it were they who were filming the morning. Down broad St Giles street it was empty enough for Anne-Marie to walk right down the middle of the lanes, tip-toeing as though the tarmac was still sleeping. She stepped into G & Ds – it opened early – to buy a croissant, then turned, went back in, and ordered two more, just in case, just because she was able to eat now. She picked them apart on the steps of the professor's house, as she listened to him in the first-floor shower.

'What are you doing here?' He'd opened the door, her back was facing him, and she turned her neck to face him – but this was too awkward a position to be doing something like this in. He gave her his hand to help her up: was there really a time when men offered women their hands like this? If there was, now wasn't the time to think about it.

'Are you going to a lecture?'

'I'm going to give the lecture.'

'What's it about?'

'Sudan.'

'OK. Let's not do this any more.'

'All right, Marie.' He rubbed the back of his head as if it was somebody else's, maybe hers. Their accents competed with one another to dominate the melody of their talk. 'Have you told David, though? That you won't have any more Arabic lessons?'

'Of *course* not.' Anne-Marie's voice was at a sort of high-tide in the morning.

'Well . . . poor David.'

'Why poor David now?' She was too tired for all of this, suddenly. The newness of breaking up with a fifty-nine-year-old had given way to the staleness of the morning, the imperfect dialogue, her unbrushed teeth.

'Never mind. But poor David will be sad.' He walked past her without awkwardness, a trick he may have mastered with a woman in Cairo or New York, in the fifties or last year, and he walked, without awkwardness, down the streets Marie had come by. Anne-Marie went back to bed, stomach full, dreaming lightly about the times in Sudan with her young hair chopped off.

*Dear Samson,*
*I wrote you a letter many years ago. I never sent it because I didn't*
*know where to find you.*


During the day:


The men here are lecherous
As the sunshine, and my legs
Are browning in shades.
The women slap my bare arms
In the market
I like it
When the UN tanks
Pass by my window
Like clouds
All dreamy and pointless.


During the day:


The city and I share sections
Of the sun with one another

Like passing segments of an orange:
    As a car-door opens
    As I comb my hair.
This is how I betrayed you
In the margins of the mornings:
Asking the creases in the curtains
    What is its secret
    Where is it weak?


I don't know where to begin:

It's always the moment when you choose to
Spread yourself into the city
Preciously, like breaking bread,
Like many suns rising from hills.
With no more need for praying then
Than artefacts need birthday-cakes,
Like a split fruit, birthing seeds:
    You open up your body's borders,
    You're your most secret state.
(It is how to die with those you hate.)


During the day:

I sent out a letter
To meet you, to warn you,
To stroke your long hair homeward:
Away from the walls that await you.
But it went astray. And feeling through valleys,
It woke, rebuked, the drunken spy-planes,

Shared sand with the kitchens of Jaffa.
You went astray. And it couldn't find you
Honey-kissing, your famous weakness:
Comparing the tones of the local women.


During the day:

You did not know where to find me.
You did not know where to look.
Either in the fields, or hiding from
both armies, or else lost in
The white pillars, built
between the letters, that
hold up the meaning of the word.
But because you came to me at night,
And you called me Delilah, of-the-night,
You left unread in my sent hot breath
What happened during the day.

*So I loved you, if that's what you're asking. Why do you have to believe I didn't? Do you need to think I am the opposite of God and of goodness? That I'm a living utter lacking of the light? You saw me only as dark, as the Song of Songs says, and don't think that you're the first to dream like that – the woman on the one hand and the Father on the other. It leaves much space in which to be a man.*

*I stood for the flesh: in your naming of things, in your alphabet, that's what my name and my figure, carved in caves, or tubed in neon for the fronts of Tel Aviv strip-clubs, would come to always stand for. It was never a name that I ever used myself. But you always called me Delilah: the same three syllables as perfect* strangers would. At least it wasn't my father's name, is what I try to remind myself when I think about it: I'm rare, by the Book, for that, and it's funny, I've always felt more like a son than a daughter.

And rarely, for something as worthless as a girl's name or a girl, Delilah still means the same thing now, in at least two warring tongues. Of the night: it's what it meant then, too, and it is what is meant by the name Layla. It was a name that made me a person of only one time. It made me a person of only one thing. It is not even which thing that I've always objected to: but what did all these men think that I did with myself the rest of the time?

You could have answered them: I wasn't of the night at all. We were at our best in the mornings. Let us get up early, as the song of songs goes, let us get up early to the vineyards; let us see if the vine flourishes, whether the tender grape appears, and the pomegranates bud forth: there I will give thee my loves.

My loves. This is what we did from the morning on, and every morning after, while the sun was still trying to catch up with us: hunting like harts, numerous as bee-swarms – swimming with my beloved, who feedeth among the lilies.

Set me as a seal upon thine heart, the song goes, as a seal upon thine arm, with your left hand under my head and your right hand embracing me. Your lips drop as the honey-comb; as a piece of pomegranate are thy temples within thy locks.

I can't remember the rest of the song, or I remember each part but in no kind of order. I remember I was singing it in my head as you slept for the final time. The verse of the knock on the door. Which I sang to the tune of the knock on my door. I sang myself silently senseless, as the men came storming in. The voice of my beloved knocketh, saying: Open to me, my sister, my love,

my undefiled: for my head is filled with dew and my locks
with the drops of the night.

*I sang silently to your lovely sleepy darkness the song's final
lines:* Make haste, my beloved, and be thou like a young hart
on the mountain of spices.

*We rarely met at night, you remember. Or, I hope that you do.
In fact I spent most my evenings in a library, trying to unlearn all
of my philistinism. I taught myself at least seven languages, as
many as one day the queen of Egypt would, grinding myself into
dust at the desk, trying to make myself as old and as wise as your
name. As a kind of a wife, as I thought I was, I thought that your
name could be a passport for the both of us.*

*But I wasn't allowed to enter into the priestly lecture theatre,
even through my body's close association with your sacred-thoughts.
All the theology books were off-limits to me. You were only half in
that Nazarite world yourself, a bright and lazy pupil, and you
skipped too many divine conversations to spend more of your mornings chasing me through the olive trees. When the time came for
you to join the holy family business, everyone knew you were going
to ditch me for some Jackie Onassis. I remember I'd been warned
by people on both sides of the war.*

*You wanted to want to learn, and you had to practise your
studiousness. So you thought that if you pushed me away from you,
you'd push the half of yourself away that thought through touch,
breathed feverish dreams, and exhausted us both with wine-
flavoured kisses. I represented the flesh. And so I was thrown from
the deck, like an empty bottle. You thought you would no longer feel
so sea-sick at being half flesh and half full of God-thoughts. What
crushed you as you ground at the mill in your blindness, and ground
on top of the women at the temple, was that you still had all of you
inside you. Your heart hadn't been cast out from your life along
with me. You were your mind. You were your flesh.*

Or perhaps you always knew that something so simple could not be true. People are not tossed coins, not even the eleven hundred coins they offered me to kill you, and since you felt like you were more than one side you must have guessed that I did too. I was of flesh but I was of my mind too. That was why you hated that I could speak those languages, wasn't it? You could pretend that it was love that made you stop my practising tongue with your practised kisses, but really I know you would have stopped me with anything. You hated that I was learning, changing. You hated that I might also talk to God.

Did you really think I didn't believe in God? You turned yourself away from me in order to face him fully. But everyone here has taken our turn in holding the hand of the African wife of St Augustine: a poor woman it is abandoned for only an idea. Even God has taken the night-watch in caring for those who faith has left itchy and widowed and soft.

It is not not-believing to have a different argument against God to the quarrel that you had with him. Try to follow me Samson – I tried my best to follow you. Why is a different way of worshipping worse than not hearing his words at all? It seems to offend you more than a loss of faith would.

You can't know me until you know what he does to me. This is probably harder for you to understand than most people: for you, a person had to get to know you by looking beyond God's powers acting upon you. But both ways are true. You have to look beyond the Delilah that laughed at your Godliness, woke you up nosily, pressed you angrily with love and hard kisses. God moved in me too. How else could I have loved you?

It is not the same argument as yours, but still I have my argument with God, my own argument, and still too I sing to him, about you, about him, when I am sleepy and happy. So tell the saints when you meet them in the book-stacks closed to the general readers: I can live as much among the word as you and still like to go swimming all day.

# CHETH

'At midnight I will rise to give thanks unto thee'

And so it came to pass that Anne-Marie wouldn't meet with the professor any more, and she took courses about the effects of colonialism, to learn how to deal with finding yourself suddenly free. David's lessons continued as normal, and they both tried to apply themselves to Arabic. Talk of a war in Iraq spread like prophecy or perfume, and aware of all the soundness of Mohammad's advice, Marie took to reading the news. And in her lazy post-colonial studies, she began to reach an understanding with empire: reconciled herself with the fact it was evil, it was in her blood, and that yet the clothes of nineteenth century explorers were more beautiful than anything. She loved both the first, colonialist, Richard Burton, and his wife who burnt his work. It seemed that in their marriage, the sins and the gifts to the world balanced out, then retreated from the world altogether. She saw in these two old explorers something vaguely like her vague self and David: learning for nothing, shining for nothing, never really understanding the world beyond their little visions – which was wrong and which was perfect.

The first Richard Burton, she read, had said that only the first thirteen languages are hard: after that you pick them up like colds. The first Richard Burton had taught himself over thirty – enough to fill a wardrobe – and all the scripts so finely woven, old Vedas and Arabic overlaid stories, they were, to Marie, like the alpha names of Givenchy and Chanel. She wanted to see how they'd fit her: her current, provisional voice felt like some nudity or sheerness. She wanted to find the perfect language for her – the second skin that had evaded her, parentless, in her odd-sounding youth. And so she began trying to teach herself as many languages as she could: Greek, Italian, Russian, not German, and a little Turkish. She just wanted to get through the first thirteen foreign tongues, and the finite borders buoyed her single-mindedness: she took to sitting in the battlements every night, running through the verb charts. She left a silent note for her later self in these quiet moments, that when you are trapped in the vastness of the world, or when you are trapped in your house, remember at least there are only so many shapes you can make with your mouth.

She started with Greek, and it all felt like roots, all earthy and dirty, and words over-ripe. In Italian and Spanish, the words were too watery, planted in the foreign soil: flavourless watermelons. Yet Turkish felt only like stroking fine crystals, clear and defined, but not yours, and indigestible. And because if you learn Greek, you must learn Turkish – and if you learn Turkish, you must learn Armenian – Western Armenian tasted like memories: it smelt like a smell you should know but you don't. It was someone else's reference-point: all the vocabulary listed in the Armenian book were words she'd never use, not in any language. And then Farsi curled up on itself before her, like looped springs on grape-vines, as though its feelers, vague feelers, held on to walled gardens, forbidden to her. In Kurdish, she couldn't get past the smell of the ergatives, and any languages after that only tasted like other languages, as if they were new girls set down before an old Casanova – as though she'd inherited an appetite from another world, and the words of this one only served to make her more hungry, for something that she'd never tasted. And so she went back to eating jelly-beans and reading *Vogue* in the library.

\*

And then it was that David, upon implicit instruction from a professor, had the idea to join the protest march against the waiting war, the march on the day after Valentine's Day. He woke the other two up, very early, and the three of them made their sleepy way to London, Mohammad having to shake Marie and David awake – but Mohammad-gently – as they slept softly upon one another. They reached Hyde Park as the sun began to shine.

They came up from the tube station and into the gathering groups: rows and rows of tables selling Socialist Worker newspapers, huddles of entire sixth-form colleges who had paid for their own coach-trip down from Peterborough or Glasgow or somewhere else, platform-heeled pink giants in fairy costumes, re-using the outfit they had worn to last summer's pride parade. But mostly, swathes of the sort of person that you'd imagine, that Marie had imagined, and dreaded, and who would wear corduroy.

And as the three ventured closer, the crowds nudged at them, like shoreline waves, lapping at a whale up-ended by the sea. Mohammad carried their hastily-put-together food and drink for the day. David carried a fairly sensible anti-war placard, compared to the 'Make Tea Not War' slogans of the other students, or the poster on sale that day that turned the blue Star of David into a swastika. Marie carried nothing, and wore a kind of low-backed black dress and sunglasses.

Everybody journeyed towards Trafalgar Square, heaving together. Marie tripped over and none of the assembled tried to help her. She decided not to like their little march: she hated the dirt of London anyway. Couldn't they let the war go on in peace? She forgot she'd be seen as marching with them, by any onlooker or camera. Forgot they'd only represent one thought. She walked backwards for a little bit, so that she could talk face-to-face with Mohammad and her boyfriend. This gave her the best view of these clusters of malcontents, tinged with lentils and a lack of imagination in her pristine view. She liked to watch how this earnest crowd had to pretend not to hear the occasional cries of 'Victory to Saddam!'

They descended on the square. Mohammad carried Marie's high heels for the last stretch, as she tiptoed through the litter that environmental activists had left. The speakers began one by one to address the crowd. Marie leant her head on David's shoulder. She was too short to see.

'Tony Benn's a legend, isn't he?'

'I wish he'd sort out his hair.'

They listened to the offerings. One of the speakers – she thought it was George Galloway – came on and shouted 'Assalamu Alaikum!' and Marie was surprised how the whole crowd knew to reply with 'Wa Alaikum Assalam!' It wasn't that she thought she was the only one who'd learnt a new tongue to deal with their new century. Perhaps it was the fact that there were English people who could speak any other language at all.

A speaker standing on the side of the fountain, after those on the platform had finished, finally said the phrases that Marie had suspected would be said from the moment she saw the banners with the Star of David joined by an '=' sign to a swastika. 'This war is a Zionist war!' The voice called into the crowds. 'This would not be happening if it wasn't for Zionist Israel! Why else do you think that Bush and Blair want to get a foot in the Middle East? Why else are they taking on a large Arab nation? They're trying to take over the whole region for the Zionist fascist pigs!'

Marie watched as people cheered. She watched to see if the man would fall into the fountain, but he didn't, and no God sent lightning for His or her amusement. She looked closely at David's face: he didn't seem shaken by this. She'd been planning to talk to him about the Stars of David swastikas, about how embarrassing it was to share an opinion with people so second-rate and so strangely focused. But now she saw that this was another thing over which the professor's influence meant she should keep silent. She turned to Mohammad for a look of Mohammad-sanity, but he was too busy trying to juggle the shoes and bags she'd made him hold for her.

'The word Trafalgar comes from Arabic, you know,' said David as he turned on his feet to get a panoramic view of the gathering. In the same way as his mother rarely sat through a television programme – from sports to cooking to art documentary – without chiming out to the sitting room '*he's* Jewish' ('Er, yeah I know, Mum, it's Chief Rabbi

Jonathan Sacks,' David's brother once had to reply), so the world was now filled with things of mysteriously Arabic origin, waiting patiently to be seen and enumerated by one young David Cohen: from mathematics, and fairy stories, to the Colombian pop star Shakira. It had become impossible to go with him to a supermarket, or to HMV.

The sun had risen to its highest point. The crowd mainly faced the same way. Perhaps as they'd marched it had looked heroic – the flow of the thousands all walking as one – although even then this would be spoilt with London's problem that there's no vantage point to observe from on high, except Buckingham Palace's balcony.

In any case, now they were stopped still, shifting from foot to foot in the spring breeze, the gathering managed to look pathetic despite its size, and the colours that they were all awash with were these: green and brown and grey. Their queasy-green placards brandished in every direction, the crowd clashed within itself like a muddy shipwreck. The colour that the Stop The War coalition had chosen for their banner was the same mossy shade as the Hamas flags that everyone had seen paraded on TV in news reports from Gaza. And their slogan: 'Not In My Name.' Not that it made any difference. Marie did not know or need their names, and Mohammad had nothing to say to them or anyone.

But David was, clearly to everyone, in his element in the crowd, like a sailor who dreams of bad seas. When the speeches were over, there was some cloud cover, and the crowd began to break into different activities he danced with London students to their tinny CD copies of the first Libertines album, and made lovely faces at the face-painted children, who in twenty years would remember the weeks before the bombs fell on to Baghdad as a time of fetes and glorious feasting.

David danced in the Trafalgar Square fountain, danced in the sun, unarmed, and with his arms out. In the way that boys and men dance without the aid of women: both light and limb-filled. Both beaming and attuned to embarrassments, his peripheries pulling him out and then his centres pulling him back in. He bordered shyness but was not occupied by it, moved to and by a conversation with himself, like a small fish flummoxed by the heave of the ocean. Gummy-smiling and dancing in the Trafalgar Square fountain to the Libertines' songs – with his dancing came his face: the place where he could hide from the ugly crowds that had surrounded him. He couldn't be held responsible for his followers that day, for what people did in his name and moist, tall shadow or under the effect of his shape. An old woman came up to David as he jumped out of the fountain, with the strangers who had joined him. 'Hello there, now I just wondering, this is my first march, so could you tell me: when does the marching actually begin?' He smiled at her brilliantly and they shared their stories of what had made them come here. Then he went back to dancing.

Anne-Marie and Mohammad sat on the cold granite walls, leg-swinging, then, when the police dispersed, climbed up to sit by the Trafalgar Square iron lions.

'I wonder what's inside it.' Anne-Marie tried to climb the side of one of the sleeping hard statues.

'It's probably hollow,' said Mohammad, nervous, and looking out for police.

'I bet it's not.' She asked for her shoes back and kicked it to hear what noise it'd make. A Biblical lion, made of iron, or full of honey: she wanted to be like that. But Mohammad had to rub her crippled toes afterwards as she sobbed, only for herself, and David waved and alpha-smiled from the fountain.

'I'm going to go and lie down on the steps of the Canadian Embassy.'

'Marie, don't be silly, things aren't that bad.'

'But it's only up the road.'

And as the evening drew on, and the music changed, David tried to get back to his bored (one patient, one impatient) friends, but was hijacked at every turn by somebody who wanted to talk about the war, or else wanted to dance with him in the fountain. David was so bright and so tall in these scenes, that he'd always either be asked to take a picture, or to pose in one with a group of strangers. He's out there in so many photo albums of strangers, tacked to many walls and fridges, his smile bobbing up just everywhere, like so many dead after a Biblical or other kind of flood, and his skin looking paler than ever, from the various exposures. He was still glowing from the day as he patiently rubbed Marie's feet on the train back home.

*

And then, of course, preface-less, the war broke out in Iraq. Perhaps after all the partying about it, it would've been a let-down any other way. And so it was that Anne-Marie lay on the bed with an unopened book in her hand.

'David, can you help me with my essay?'

He sighed and pushed the sleeves of his shirt up. 'I'm not going to be able to help you when you're in the exam hall, Annie.'

'Fine. I'll call Mohammad.'

'What? He'll be asleep.'

'He won't mind.'

'That's not the point.'

'Mohammad's nice to me.'

'Oh, for fuck's sake.'

The next day, she gave up on her studies, and put the notes she'd made into her hat-boxes. And so she learnt that procrastination was as wide a terrain as sex – like sex or faith: no narrative, no simple sentences, with beginnings-and-endings, could convey the endless hours, the varied texture, the utter devotion to the act. Only she was an expert. She could have written the equivalent of the Gospels, the *Kama Sutra*, or Wikipedia for the brainless and the lazy. If only she could have been bothered. Instead she filled her days with walking around thinking about all the things she could be doing.

It was also around this time that Marie began to pretend to be a writer. Writers probably walked around a lot pretending to be thinking, so that could be her job. There was a beautiful half-Indian girl with alpha cheekbones who ran Oxford's creative-writing group, and Anne-Marie would follow her around the bookshop on her shifts, looking at what titles she picked up. She even began to attend the cheekboned-girl's writing evenings, and she'd sit in a corner, filling three plastic chairs with her legs and possessions, feeling miserable for being the only person (in the room; in the world) not in the midst of creating 'Edward Said! The Musical' or 'Subcomandante Marcos: A devised piece in five acts.' And when even this pretending came to be too much hard work, she took to following any half-famous Oxford writer, from Thom Yorke to Philip Pullman, through the

Jericho streets like so many fictional murderers. She told the university she was dropping out after spending a week trying to get Mohammad and David to help her follow a man she was convinced was the missing Manic Street Preacher guitarist, Richey Edwards. She moved all her things, which were not hers, into David's room, and sat there cutting out pages of Italian *Vogue*.

*

And then the friends and a few English girls they approved of went night-swimming in the river, just before David and Mohammad's exams, bringing beer and still-warm bread, David jumping off bridges, laughing ferociously, scaring everyone, as Marie was left to steer the wooden boat that they'd found in a graduate college. She silently implored Mohammad at least to look at the English girls.

David told them there that he'd made up his mind to go to Palestine. Marie chose to follow him loyally: this was easy to do because she had no money. She would pack his suitcases for him, deciding what to leave behind. She would let David be the one to say goodbye to the professor.

'But you'll die,' said one of the English girls.

'You'll die if you don't put some more layers on.' Everyone was shivering by now from the exposed and cloudless sky. Mohammad looked as if he didn't know what to say, and tidied up the empty beer cans in the boat.

'You'll visit us, won't you Mohammad?'

'Of course.' His face did a funny painful smile. 'Of course. Will you come and visit me?'

Mohammad was going to Geneva. After he got the top mark in his year for law, David encouraged him to write to human rights groups for paid internships. Marie was very excited at the prospect of the stationery Mohammad might encounter, and send to her, from the United Nations departments. But they were all very sad to be separated: it felt as if their conversations with each other had not even begun.

\*

And so it was again that Mohammad looked as if he didn't know what to say, when David, on the last night, the two of them swimming together, said: 'Europe's over, it failed us, it's finished.'

'But what are you actually going to do there?'

'The professor's wanted to set up a library in the West Bank for a while – a mix of Arabic books and books that colleges here don't need any more. He said he wants someone to oversee it in the first stages, and it might turn into a centre for teaching English and French.'

'Do you agree with that?' he asked neutrally.

'With what?'

'Teaching the Palestinians English and French. I don't know, I just thought . . . when we've spoken about it, you always said it sort of missed the point to . . .'

'The professor says it's not neo-colonial. It's about giving them power. Giving them English gives them more weapons to fight with. It's still a subversive act,' he said.

'What about teaching them French?'

'Yeah. That's probably pretty pointless.'

'Maybe he said it to give Marie something to do,' Mohammad said quietly.

David dived under the water in response.

They got out of the river after an hour, put the rest of their clothes on, drank half a bottle of whisky by the deserted punt hire shop, and ran around the ancient streets to try to warm themselves up. The alcohol caught up with them as they began to jog. They stopped and jumped up and down at the end of the walled street by New College. Mohammad bumped himself from one wall to the other.

'You're like a dust-cart.'

'Roland Barthes was killed by a dust-cart.'

'Khan, I *am* that dust-cart,' David rammed himself into Mohammad's side.

'No, Cohen, *I'm* that dust-cart.' Mohammad slammed back and hit David's shoulder with his.

'I'm the dust-cart. You're the filth.'

'*You're* the filth.'

They crashed into each other's sides with all their force. David slammed into the right wall, then bounced back hard enough to slam Mohammad into the left wall with his hip.

They both fell, lying on the ground, laughing and panting.

'Oi, Khan, get up, you twat.'

'Oy, Cohen, but I can't.'

They lay in the gutter for a little while longer.

'Do we even use the word "dust-cart" in this country?'

'No, Khan, we do not.'

'What do we use instead? Like pavement for sidewalk?'

'Um . . . I'm not really sure.'

PART TWO

# TETH
'Teach me good judgement and knowledge'

When David and Marie landed at Ben Gurion Airport and got through the questions at the passport control, David held Marie's hand so hard and happy that she thought she might have to stop him from running up to the soldiers and throwing his arms around them in an undiscerning act of love. The war was here and so their life was, in all its new, young-smelling freedom: it followed that a little part of him must have loved the war itself. His hair shone in the sun, his smile began vividly smiling; Anne-Marie had to take her shoes off to keep up with his happy step.

Marie didn't much question the idea that this would be their life now. She'd never graduated, and so it was as if the final parenthesis hadn't closed upon her affected adolescence: she could as easily pretend to be an international volunteer worker as she could pretend to be an Oxford student. She didn't query David's desire to walk into a war-zone, and her immortal brain was successfully hardwired against imagining the danger they might encounter here. Nor did she wonder at his choice of Palestine: she'd grown used to hearing it in conversations with the professor, and the mysterious reported exchanges that took place between the professor and David. As for how this fitted in with David's Jewish background, her liberal instruction had long since taught her to repeat: *a person is the label that they choose to use themselves*. She was just happy that they'd be able to lie in the sun and not wake up too early.

And so it was that they were met outside the airport by Ricardo, an Italian man in his thirties, who'd come to the West Bank after writing his PhD on the Situationists. He seemed to have been working his way through war-zones alphabetically, so whether he was counting the 'P' for Palestine, or the 'W' for West Bank, he must have been quite a veteran to be here. David trusted him and his systematic conflict-zone credentials. Marie didn't like the way he looked at her.

It had been arranged that Ricardo would drive them to where he stayed in East Jerusalem, where he ran language classes, and sat in ambulances to stop them getting fired at by the Israelis – 'on the grounds that there are valuable Western people inside them'. Was he just imitating what Israelis thought? What he thought Israelis thought? The way he said it, it seemed to Marie a little as if he thought it was true: we're Western, we *are* more valuable.

At Ricardo's house in East Jerusalem, they were introduced to the Westerners who worked nearby – mainly Scandinavians, some Americans, some Canadians, with very faded T-shirts, and a funny sort of smell – who ran some of the various charity projects and NGOs in Palestine. They took Marie and David under their wing, and the two were duly ungrateful.

David explained their plans in the West Bank. They want to set up a library, they said (he said); they can work with the International Solidarity Movement too, they said (he said), sitting in ambulances to help them through the checkpoints, or wearing ugly bright clothes in front of bull-dozers. Anne-Marie blocked the terror of these outfits from her mind with talk of the occupation.

After a beer or two, Ricardo drove them to the town where they'd be living, just past East Jerusalem, just past everything. They passed the falling-down houses that had been there since the British left, and the temporary-looking buildings that had been used for forty years. Driving past the off-green stretch of olive groves that greeted them before their town, Ricardo played a guessing game about a rusting tank that sat in a field. 'Maybe '67. I don't think '73.'

The building that was to be the library was born out of a side-cracked Mandate-era house that a rich Christian family had left, and which a local imam had been taking care of until the professor struck up a deal to convert it into a community project. Two Swedish volunteers had begun to take in the book deliveries and buy collections of Arabic textbooks, but had left to work in Afghanistan in early 2002.

The top-most floor was to be their private quarter, and the internal walls of the downstairs rooms had been knocked down. Now the vast single room was half-way through being converted into corridors of bookshelves. Anne-Marie looked forward to watching David dragging the bookcases into place, and she'd begun to make the deci-sions about which branches of knowledge would go where.

There could be nothing better in the world than living in a library. From their childhoods and their time at Oxford, they just needed books nearby – not to read or understand, just the comfort and the smell of them, the way that those who've grown up by a beach always need to live where they can hear the roar of the sea.

'Casanova was a librarian, you know,' Marie said as they ate their first meal on their knees in the filth of the downstairs emptiness.

'So were a lot of ugly people.'

'Come on, let's see what it looks like if we push all the shelves against the wall, and put all the chairs in the middle.'

'I'm tired, Annie.'

'I just wanted to see.'

Anne-Marie and David slept in a corner of the downstairs room on the first night, under blankets, arguing harmlessly about when to do what, with books at their feet and making love to the sound of the faint gunfire. Marie felt safe in David's moral certainty, in those first heated nights in the almost-war-zone, and it's true that his arms had grown quickly strong from moving the rubble that had seemingly grown organically, like concrete weeds, on the pathway to their house.

They spent their first week meeting their neighbours. Anne-Marie opened her mouth, and was told that she spoke a wrong kind of Arabic – the professor hadn't mentioned the cultural-imperialism of the Egyptian dialect he'd taught her. Marie kept her mouth shut from then on. She sat, bored-looking, like an archetype of obnoxious-western-girl-for-hire, at the edge of any table in any house in the town. David spoke animatedly to the family who had invited them in for dinner, as they told him – in an accent that Marie couldn't understand – about their youngest son's death at the hands of an Israeli sniper, and about their eldest son's love of Manchester United.

Marie's new hobby was watching David play football with the boys in the village, in the alley of broken pipes and a sanitation unit, which could be seen from the side window of the library.

David's new hobby was to watch and help Anne-Marie take afternoon-long baths, now that she had no shower to purify herself with, or to shower with David in, as they'd done in Oxford, laughing and washing each others' hair. The bathroom was large and peeling and chipped; the bathtub was iron and white ceramic. David pulled it out into the middle of the room. They had to fill it up with hot water from the tank in the kitchen. David would run backwards and forwards for hours, topping it up when it got cold. Once he slipped with a pail of water and hit his head on the floor, and Marie pretended that it was a war wound.

\*

It took three weeks to get the library ready. They compiled a list of the stock left by the Swedish volunteers, then David went to a Jerusalem internet café to tell the professor what gaps needed filling. Ricardo brought these new stocks around almost immediately, and soon there were Arabic books on how to learn French, French books on the principles of feminism, English novels, poetry in every language, and a number of books they both knew they'd have to be physically forced to read. This was their ideal hostage situation: be held up by a group of charming Palestinian men, get David's parents to pay the ransom, but only after a few weeks in which they'd been made, at gunpoint, to practise their foreign languages and read French philosophy.

David pushed the shelves into thin rows on one side of the vast room, and bought rosy-red comfortable chairs for the reading area. Anne-Marie polished the floor, in her short blue-striped dress and red headscarf. They argued over whether sociology and anthropology were the same: Marie's secret system was to put any analytical book on Africa under Anthropology, and any studies on the West under Sociology. She told David this, and they shouted about colonial-thinking, then made up, and lay on the wet floor. Afterwards, as Anne-Marie was changing into a clean dress, she picked up a book in one of the remaining boxes, and put it under poetry.

'Rumi belongs under Islam,' David argued.

But she read out some lines: 'It's love poetry. The biggest-selling love poet in America,' she said, though she couldn't remember where she'd read this. But they were tired of arguing and making up again, so she took the book into their bedroom, where it wouldn't need to be defined. She'd read it in bed sometimes when they had nothing else to do, reading it out the way she used to read out pages from French Vogue, in a voice of nothing, but still a timbre coolly outlined against the sweating of the night.

*

Then from the day that the library opened, all the Palestinian girls in the town fell deep in love with David. They called him Justin Timberlake, because of his smile and his stupid boyish jeans, and for the wonders that privations and Ramadan had begun to do for his tall hip-bones.

Marie didn't ask by what great miracle a people who sometimes had to go without running water could know about American pop stars. She observed the headscarf-clad girls impartially, as they came in to browse the books and to see if David would come out of the upstairs bathroom and on to the mezzanine landing in his towel. But David was too culturally sensitive for just about anybody's liking: they only saw any shade of his bareness when he politely took off his shoes inside their homes.

And so it was that, some mornings, they'd hear youthful giggling from outside their window and look out to see a flowerbed of teenage smiles and scarves and eyelashes. Other times, they'd be waiting for the girls all day, and would only later hear either (good news): that the schools were running as normal, or (bad news): there was a 'martyr's' funeral later that week, for which they all had to prepare.

When David was out playing football with their brothers, the village girls and Anne-Marie tiptoed towards a kind of connection. There was a set-back when she admitted she'd never been to a Justin Timberlake concert, and she didn't know whether she preferred Britney Spears to Cristina Aguilera. But eventually one of the taller girls conceded to Marie that she could be a pop star too.

'Really? OK . . . um . . .' It was such an honour that it deserved careful thought. 'Can I be Shakira?' A chorus of laughter ruled this out. 'Beyoncé?'

'But you are blonde.'

The older girl looked her up and down. 'You can be Madonna.'

'But she looks like a witch these days.' Marie refused to disguise her disappointment. But it turned out that the Palestinians had not received the news of Madonna Ciccone's ageing: maybe this was how an occupation affects the local culture, Anne-Marie thought. Things the professor had taught her to say came back to her, even now – at every inappropriate moment.

\*

And so, unable to forge links with the girls, the families, anyone, Marie chose to explore the surroundings: the olive groves and the paths that stopped suddenly at the edges of the town. But like the language available to describe female desire, the language and maps for an in-road into the politics and death of the landscape all felt false to her and not her own. So Anne-Marie would have to be a pioneer. Which she didn't mind: she'd a bought a khaki Dior dress just before they'd flown out, and had set her sights on the aviator sunglasses the soldiers wore at the border. At least she'd look lovely for herself, she decided, walking the parts where the other girls had stopped.

Only, the first time she ventured out of the street she lived on, and on to the sweaty, parchment-coloured roads on the edge of the town, Ricardo drove past her in his old white car and said:

'Maria, get in immediately.'

In her glorious arrogance she guessed this was some sort of sexual invite, to be played out against a foreign landscape for added effect, or to excuse it afterwards. She stopped, and frowned when Ricardo said: 'I'm not a-joking Maria. Girls can't walk round here by themselves. Don't try to make a point. You'll end up getting raped.'

Even to the internationals then, the others were the rapists, dark and in dark corners, waiting for her without love – and if Marie wasn't scared at that, still she was scared of Ricardo's face then, when he said it. She was scared of the word rape from the mouths of Italians, in Italian: Italian the language of love – scared that love and opposites now would perhaps all have to pass through the same, narrow passage. So there was no language of exploration for her. If there had been, it was replaced with Ricardo's accent upon that word. David walked with her from now on, but she usually let him go out alone. Marie would go for whole days without leaving the library. She'd go through whole afternoons without leaving the bathtub.

*

David and Marie would sleep in all morning: no one used the library then, unless the Israeli soldiers turned the children back from school. Things were, they were told, unusually quiet. Only one boy from the village had been shot, while running across a checkpoint, since the two had arrived. Marie liked to think that they had brought the place good luck. Sadly they also brought the place *the internationals*.

All the activists in the West Bank, especially those working with the International Solidarity Movement, had heard about the library, probably from Ricardo, or else some contact 'back there' [insert thumb-pointing-over-shoulder hand gesture], such as the professor. The professor seemed to have a lot of contacts here.

They took it upon themselves to pay each other visits

whenever possible, and so came a succession of parties, at the instigation of others, where they'd sit round on the roof of the library, listening to Arcade Fire's first album or the three other CDs that they had between them, and comparing tales about the illegal tactics of the IDF. They would've compared scars, if only they'd had any.

For the most part the Palestinians were quote-unquote 'Palestinians', revered and held at arm's length by the internationals, and, as such, few were invited or came to these parties. The internationals told themselves that it was out of respect – it was true that they drank a lot of wine and took anything illegal that Ricardo could pick up in Jerusalem: measly amounts of soft drugs bought from gap-year kibbutzniks and rationed out like the Blitz.

But once or twice Ricardo brought along his friend from East Jerusalem, a bright-eyed electrician with sticking out ears, called Mohammad. And so it was that Anne-Marie got to talking to him on the roof, as David sorted out their temperamental CD player, because she couldn't stand any more of the international's gruesome stories: of massacres in Jenin, of rapes in Bethlehem. Mohammad the electrician almost won her friendship, when they stalled upon his name. It was so unlike a story to have two friends called the same thing, and two Mohammads doubly tricky, triply tricky, more. The early Muslim societies might've variously claimed Mahdiship for Muhammad ibn Isma'il, Muhammid ibn al-Hanafiyya, and other, minor, hyphen-ibn Muhammads, let in generously through the side-doors of gnostic influences, but still this didn't mean Marie could so easily let lesser Mohammads into the holy family of her friendship. It was hard for her to let him be his own self, without imposing her ideas and memories of the other boy that she'd known in England. But this Mohammad smiled too expertly, threw his head back laughing so perfectly, to not be liked for long. The triumph of her brief humanity came when he told Marie that he couldn't swim, unlike the other Mohammad, and she believed him. She still tried to push him in a river during one of their walks, though.

Anne-Marie made sure this Mohammad came to their parties from then on, if he didn't have trouble travelling there. He had no phone, so at every party she told him the date for the next one. She introduced him to David while he was sanding a desk with Ricardo's machinery. She called him Mohammad N., or M.N., and then Eminem, for short, and Eminem, Justin Timberlake and Madonna became the trinity of the roof-parties. She thought it was her duty to correct his Arabic from the colloquial 'keef haal-ek' to the modern standard 'kaef-al haal', as if to say: 'Your parents might be *Palestinians*, or whatever, and that's all very nice, but I studied Arabic at *Oxford*, you know – exactly what qualifications did your parents have when they taught you?' He would tell her she looked beautiful in a rare way that meant: he just thought it, it was an offering. She offered him more insults in response. It was a paradigm for friendship.

But Anne-Marie and David had no way of getting in touch with him, and by winter he'd stopped coming to their parties. Marie didn't question it much at first: she was just embarrassed that their parties were no good. Then after about six months without seeing him, they heard the news that a young man called Mohammad N. had been shot near East Jerusalem, but Marie couldn't be sure that it was him. Suddenly it seemed as though the world was full of Mohammads, all missing, and all impossible to pray for. She told herself that, like a Mahdi, he hadn't died, he'd gone into occultation: to return some time when the world was ready for his smile, his ears, his terrible jokes and compliments.

*

And after that Anne-Marie had only the internationals to offend, with her kafiya-miniskirts, with her goldenness and her laughter. It helped they couldn't help but be boring to her: opinions on Palestine and Israel were inflated currency here, like banknotes in Zimbabwe then, everyone's pockets crammed full of the airy worthlessness of their thoughts on the subject. They traded them like playground collectable cards as they smoked up on the roof. The internationals treated Marie and David as an indivisible unit, as if not wanting to touch upon her directly – and talking in similar blocks about themselves, they told each other their inter-changeable stories of how they'd ended up Here.

Mika and Kyla, a young couple of interchangeably inter-national origin – portions of Greek, French Jewish, and Lebanese, by way of MIT and Georgetown – were like a portrait of David and Marie, done with cheaper materials, less lovingly: dried pasta and orange lentil beans, like a child's collage made at school. Anne-Marie saw a horror of hinting in the mornings when David's once-beautiful hair was left increasingly matted as Mika's; Kyla's pinkish tan, amateurish somehow, like her skin didn't understand the situation, would make Marie sit, worrying about wrinkles, as the rest of them discussed illegal airstrikes.

Mika and Kyla, talking as a unit, told the story of the young English man who'd been shot in the Gaza Strip while they worked there. He'd been a sociology student at

Cambridge. He'd been wearing an orange boiler suit. He'd been waving a tank away from a house of children. The only time Mika and Kyla had been to England was to go to his funeral: 'It's a depressing country, isn't it?'

Marie had nothing to say in response to these stories that were brought to her in the library. To stand with your peace-flag in front of an army tank and be surprised when you get shot at: this is all the joy of youth. To demand to be fired upon, and then have all your friends be outraged for you: this is love. She thought all of this should've been obvious to them.

But it came to pass that there were other stories, from all the other Back Theres that there were, and Anne-Marie would have to sit through them all, like court proceedings on regrettable marriages between the privileged and the real. Jordan and Marc had come here together, after taking Middle Eastern Studies courses at McGill, which they some-times sheepishly mentioned they'd never actually managed to pass. Michel had come from a Paris different from Marie's – an ugly Paris of student-clothing, embarrassing student politics, seminar-rooms – where he'd been writing his PhD, before he decided the work of the International Solidarity Movement was more important. Anne-Marie agreed this was probably true, but wasn't a comment on the effectiveness of activism.

And Yoni came from Seattle. Yoni had been to Afghani-stan. Yoni and David owned a number of similar-looking T-shirts. Yoni's liberal Jewish parents agreed with what he was doing out here: '*It's not anti-Jewish to be anti-Israel,*' he chorused along to others who were elsewhere, as he drank straight from a wine bottle. And one evening, sitting on plastic garden-furniture chairs, which Ricardo had brought to put on the roof, Yoni told the other internationals his Back There story. He'd gone to Afghanistan after university, to work for a charity that was trying to get compensation from the US Government for the families of Afghan civilian casualties. In Kabul, he had fallen in love with a girl called Marla.

Anne-Marie listened with uncharacteristic patience to any story involving this girl – the way that she used to melt the hearts of American soldiers; the way she used to try to break into army camps; the parties she threw that everyone attended; the blondeness of her hair.

Yoni came to Palestine after the girl was killed during her first week in Iraq. He felt he could neither go to the countries of American wars, nor return home to Seattle. And after too much whisky, Yoni talked in cover-ups. They covered-up her death, he'd say, it was them, them, it was the Americans. He'd pound his fists: Americans, Americans, until Ricardo would bring him soothing things and David would talk to him with quiet deliberateness. But Marie, listening for once, believed for once, and wanted to, in this cover-up, prophetic cover-up, that was spoken of in drunken tongues: the final sleepy sigh of a cover-up, the one that covered the whole world. This cover-up ploughed the earth and filled it all with all of us, white-washed everything, once and for all, and divided it into airtight bags, signed for and sent to Geneva or The Hague. It was the climax everyone was looking for in PhDs or Palestine or Prada. Marie would sit in the plastic chair, lost in her thoughtlessness, thinking the name: Marla Marla Marla Marla Marla. She later heard that there was going to be a Hollywood film made about this girl, and her Afghan war parties. It was going to be filmed in Nevada and Marla would be played by Kirsten Dunst.

\*

And then it was that David and the other internationals permitted Marie one day trip into Jerusalem, in the hope that it would stop her romanticising it. Getting into Palestine for the first time, David and Anne-Marie had only seen the city through Ricardo's car window, and were both so nervous about crossing the border that they barely took in the view of the valleys and monuments. Marie kept asking questions about its beauty and its age, accidentally saying its name in conversations, whenever she could, like a schoolgirl with a crush.

'When did they raze the walls of the city? When did that treaty hand it over to the prince of Germany? Why do they like General Allenby – wasn't he English? Why would they like that?'

'You're not at Oxford now,' they'd say, as though questions were reserved for places that had Victorian fireplaces. They all took the tone of discouraging a young girl against an unsuitable, scruffy boyfriend, until David sulkily agreed to meet this good-for-nothing city in dark glasses.

'It's one lousy day, David, it's not going to kill you.'

'I wouldn't make you do something that made you uncomfortable.'

'You're fucking joking, right?' She waved her arms around to indicate *Palestine*.

'I didn't even ask you to come here,' David said slowly through his teeth.

And so it was that they borrowed a *Lonely Planet Guide* from one of the internationals knowing that the whole day Marie and David were away, the internationals back in the library would argue over whether it was acceptable even to own a tourist guide to Israel, or a *Lonely Planet Guide* to anywhere, and stood in a hostile hexagon round a table, in a verbal Mexican hold-up, the word 'neo-colonialist' pointed to each person's head.

Anne-Marie's passing elbow in the car was spat at by an Israeli soldier on the border; her uncovered ankles were spat at by an Arab woman in Jerusalem. There was a certain democracy to it. They parked Ricardo's car and worked their way up to the walled old city in the heat, and sat down against the familiar-looking medieval battlements to choose where to go from the tourist-book.

But everything in the world was out of the question for them. No museums – in this lovely weather; no more mosques – in that dress you're wearing; no birthplaces, graves, of prophets or of kings; no art galleries – The Occupation is cultural; no archaeology sites – ancient history is a weapon; no great churches and no synagogues – for either Marie or for David, not even looking from the outside.

They argued so exhaustingly that David hit his head with the book in frustration. A middle glossy page, showing a five-star hotel in Eilat, fell out and they left it there. They trudged through the gates to the old city in bitter silence, stopping only to say 'We do not speak English' to the faux-friendly tour guides, who were watching them lizardly, to offer them made-up tours on the Via Dolorosa.

Anne-Marie and David grew thirsty, refusing to be nourished by Israel. Inside the gates they both tight-jaw conceded that they needed to buy something to drink. They walked into the first café that faced out to the cobbled streets, and Marie ordered two iced coffees in her half-remembered Hebrew.

'Where did you pick that up?' David asked angrily.

'It's a language, David, not syphilis.'

'Where did you learn it?'

Marie looked at him incredulously. Her cheeks had caught a little too much sun. '*You* taught it to me. When we first met.'

'Well,' his eyes looked her up and down, 'you don't normally have such a good memory.'

'What's that supposed to mean?'

And then they'd argue again in the heat.

David stirred the straw in his drink around angrily. Thirty more minutes of clawing at each other's borders eventually yielded a choice they agreed on – the Armenian church for the brother of Jesus, who they read of for the first time over their iced coffees, a lost little saint called John the Just. They walked around the Armenian quarter but couldn't find it anywhere. Not that night, but another time, Marie had a dream about all the brothers that Jesus Christ might have had. Then the two left for Palestine, empty-handed, empty-headed, and barely able to look each other in the eye.

On the way out of the old city, Anne-Marie was shouted at by old men for taking photos of the UN cars that were parked in a row, by the Tower of David museum. She agreed to put David's camera away but wouldn't move on, embarrassing a mumbling monk, by just *looking* and *looking*. David tugged on her arm with lovely force but she kept standing there. The black UN lettering on the bright white bonnet was in a font so crisp that it was worthy of Chanel. How did they have no mud on their outsides? How did they have no people inside? She understood now why Mohammad wanted to work for the UN: the cars were so beautiful and undefiled that she wanted to climb inside one of them and go to sleep for the rest of the day and probably forever.

י

# JOD
'Let the proud be ashamed'

Eventually it grew a kind of colder, and the two began to settle in. The library's shelves changed as regularly as seasons: Marie watched unhelpfully, smiling, as David dragged the shelves into new positions, shifting connections, making new awkward bedfellows between shy books, or swearing as he dropped them on to his bare feet. They did this every few weeks – routine spread miraculously amidst the gun-fire, and they even began to dream, at night, about the place they lived in during the day. And the parties with the internationals continued every Friday. On Saturday mornings, they cleared up the wine bottles nervously but their neighbours never said anything, especially to Marie. There were still stories of when the rich Christians had lived in that house in the 1920s: the building was already marked.

During the day, she began to spend more time with the local girls, searching for the feeling of female friendship that had thus far always eluded her. The girls began to come up to her room whenever David was out, scared as they were of his beauty and height. They'd talk to Anne-Marie in English, Arabic and pop lyrics. She never learnt their names, and perhaps because of this they were fickle in their love of her: they'd happily plait her hair for her, but sometimes pull too hard on purpose. Marie felt like she constantly had to win them over, and she eked out morsels of secrets for them, as if they were paying for them in gold, about what David did when he was alone. She had no idea what David did when he was alone.

And David was alone more often these days: he'd taken Ricardo up on his offer to sit in the ambulances crossing the Israeli border. The tactic was having some effect, so they said: fewer Palestinians were being held up at the border as they bled to death these days. Anne-Marie respected that David didn't ask her to join him, but still she didn't know what to do when he came home to the library one evening, after seeing his first real-life dead body. She had to not believe it, and that night it was Marie who pushed David away. She got up in the middle of the night, to practise her dancing to Madonna's early hits, in order to impress the girls at the pretend-parties they had in the library, or all jumping on a narrow, cuddly-bear-covered bed, when David and their parents were away.

She made the mistake of telling the girls that David was feeling troubled, at one of these stuffed-toy dance parties. She didn't think of the cruelty of it: to say, the man I love can't cope because his life is a bit like yours now. The girls wanted to do something to make it better. They loved the idea that they could help him. They knocked on the library door too early one morning, shy, delighted as they were to be met with a recently bathed Cohen boy, who smiled his broadest, kindest smile, a tooth for each girl's heart.

'Come with us, we want to show you.'

Marie came to the front door with a cup of English tea, and she stood behind David, her arm around his waist.

'What are you up to, girls?'

'Come and see!'

Down in the alley, in David's honour, they had written his name out in the gunpowder they took from the Crayola-colour cartridges, left by teenage soldiers, which still littered all the village's streets. They wrote it out in Arabic, joined-up, and leant down with matches and set it alight. The fire swirled from one end to the other. It stayed aflame for a second, an endless second, then exhausted itself and fizzled out.

'Aren't you lovely! Thank you! Shukran shukran!' David hugged all the girls one by one, which he rarely did since Ricardo's lectures on respecting Muslim sensitivities. The girls hugged each other and Marie, in ripples of happiness from the original Cohen embrace. Everyone was in the mood to celebrate. Everything was sparkling and fast-flying as gunpowder. David took the day off from re-arranging the library shelves, to paint a mural with the girls on the side of the building, which is probably still there, unless they've torn the wall down by now.

And in the following weeks, the girls taught Marie how to make words out of gunpowder, although not how to hunt for cartridges, and she liked to write things out in every language she knew. But she found that each one had its own problems when it came to setting it alight: Hebrew was too chunky, Spanish too short, Turkish inconsistent, and

Arabic always too fast. She remembered all the languages she'd tried and failed to learn, in her room, in the library, in the cold and in the sun here, and they struck her now as so many shopping-lists: none of the words flared up from the dusty streets, none felt like they were real. She wondered how to find the secret language to spell out in the fire. She wanted to trick David into telling her his secret words, but these days he was usually too busy inside ambulances even to watch and make unappreciative comments, grinning from the window.

Anne-Marie spent whole afternoons in the alley, pouring out the insides of cartridges, and shaping them with her fingertips. It didn't matter to Marie what the sentences said, and she never photographed them as the trail of fire fizzed around, the way that the local girls did with David's camera. She burnt instead into her memory the phrases most suited to going up in smoke:

*Coeli enarrant gloriam Dei*

*Ya Basta*

*Yves Saint-Laurent*

The girls helped her to kneel and re-light it whenever the explosives sadly failed.

\*

But such innocence was not to last.

About nine months into the establishment of the library, one of the girls ran into the building crying, calling out for Justin Timberlake. Marie watched the scene from behind the poetry section, where her finger was grazing the titles meaninglessly. David was sitting at his desk, filling out the paperwork of the library's accounts, and calmed the girl, asking: What was it? in Arabic.

Marie's mind raced through the possibilities, starting at 'bomb' and 'body'. Earlier that week the Israeli army had come to the village next door and shot a house of militants, among them a militant eight-year-old boy with glasses. But it was none of these things. It was pornography. This was far down on her list of potential worries. But it turned out that a Scandinavian volunteer had left a dirty magazine in the home of a family, who'd invited them to stay in their house for free, who'd moved their children into one bedroom to give them enough room. The girl had found it looking for something to play with because her school was closed. She explained to David in his language – it was clear she didn't want to touch the topic with her own. *Women. Photographs. Not beautiful.* She was crying. *For men.* She fiddled with her headscarf. Sometimes she'd go from a cry to a frown: she looked like she didn't know where she should look.

And so David smiled his softest smile, more from his eyes than his mouth, and held her hand until she had stopped her initial weeping, because the questions that were to come – *Do men want that? Do they hate us? Should I tell my father?* – would be beyond Justin Timberlake's powers to answer. He seemed to try to give her space without erasing himself completely, and Marie loved him deeply in that moment, trying to find his way through the difficulty of being a man in front of girls. He sat on the edge of the desk, looking prepared to listen to whatever she said, and trying to convey that with eyes looking mostly down. But the girl didn't say much more, just cried a little and soon exhausted herself, like a gunpowder name but meaning nothing.

David walked her home to her family and her bed covered in soft toys.

David raged at the internationals over the pornography, forming his fists, mixing foul languages. He drove them out of the temple of the library, upturning their gaudy, jewelled beliefs that they were still the good guys: 'You're like a bunch of filthy teenagers. Pathetic, looking at that crap. Can't you get a real woman?' Marie stood by him faithfully. This was easy to do because she hated anything involving unflattering lighting. And life went on as before in the library, until the girl who'd found the magazines was so always-shaken and unable to sleep that she began to knock on their door, in the middle of the night – asking if she could just lie there and be held by David.

\*

Then the sound of a girl crying became their main siren and alarm clock, hard to hammer into the structure of a wider, worldwide cause to fight for. The pillows in their bedroom had all been summoned to cover Marie's ears through the night.

'David, we have to do something about this.' Anne-Marie was putting her dress back on in the darkness: the girl had been screaming outside for the last fifteen minutes. It had been happening now for three weeks, disturbing their sleep, and David worrying that the girl would get into trouble with the Israelis as well as the local authorities, for causing such disturbances. David and the girl's parents had reached a decision that she'd no longer be admitted to the library if she kept doing this. The first few nights of comforting her, milk and chocolate, stories read, had worn too thin and it was not a sweet, just-this-once moment of closeness any more: now it was a routine of exhaustion. David eyes cast down in thought. The girl's voice was shaking their fragile bedroom peace.

'We can't just leave her outside,' he said.

'I just don't understand: if it terrified her why does she want to sleep with you?'

'It confused her.'

'We're not helping her. We need to tell her to stop. I should tell her – maybe she's scared of me.'

'That's not something to be proud of, Marie.'

Marie turned the lights in the bedroom on and opened up the old, thin window. She shouted in Arabic for the girl to go away. The girl's face became some sort of terrible thing at this, and the noises terrible, like injured stray cats. David covered his face away from the outside and the girl and Marie and all else. But Anne-Marie was determined now, and ran to the bathroom to fill a ceramic pot with water. She ran back to the window and poured the water over the girl. The cries turned to shocked whimpers, and then whimpers only heard in the distance.

Marie saw David looking at him.

'What?' she put her hand on her hip.

'Marie . . .'

'I had to sleep alone when I was her age.'

David drew the palms of his hands slowly from the top to the bottom of his face. 'Jesus. Fucking. Christ. Marie,' he said quietly as he rubbed his eyes, but she had already turned the light off.

*Dear Delilah,*

*I loved you, if that's what you're asking. I loved you more than anything. And the very fact that I loved at all was a new kind of miracle to me. Loving you was the only thing that I did for myself.*

*You were my rebellion against G-d. From the time even before my birth, I had been so under the tides of his planning that I didn't know my thoughts from His, and I swept from slaying to marriage to sleeping, all upon the disquieting force from inside me, which I could never understand or look upon face-on.*

*But my love for you came forth like the wildflowers, which a field must just have, must have for it to breathe through. It was neither sowed and nor was it reaped by Him: I saw you and it simply was.*

*And from the feeling this love brought me, from this acute sense of merely existing, for the first time in my led life I saw the blunt side of the butchery He had made of my desires. He had mixed my wills with His own as bitterly as the taste of two different wines.*

*The first thing we want of any beautiful object is to put it in our mouth. And you were the only thing for me that tasted of its own flavour. He made sure that everything else out there was of Him. G-d in the wine, G-d in the honey, G-d in the fig, G-d in the* taste of a woman: I'd try to wash my tongue with water. But water tasted of G-d.

I know that you might be angry, Delilah, as you read this part of the letter. I'm bringing Him into everything again. You'll say that even when we are at our closest I'll always have another name on my tongue, that I am cheating in a crueller way than you ever did to me. And it is fair that you should be allowed to envy G-d, in the way that men do. You can't be jealous of Him like a woman while I'm trying to tell you: you were the only thing or person that I had ever chosen.

And I know that choice is not a sacrifice, but still it is a gift. Out of all the world, you were the alpha, and there were no other letters. If a force other than G-d made me love you, it was the force of freedom. In Psalm 119, which is not one of David's, it is sung: the wicked have waited for me to destroy me. Thou art my hiding-place and my shield: I hope in thy word. Thou hast trodden down all them that err from thy statues: for their deceit is falsehood. Thou puttest away all the wicked of the earth like dross: therefore I love thy testimonies. My flesh trembleth for fear of thee and I am afraid of thy judgements.

And recently a band of angels sang a prayer whose tentacles reached all the way down to my room in the library. It is the psalm of choice, of horrible freedom, and they sang it for through the smog in sorrow, on the day that the terrorists bombed London:

Inside the heart
Is the city.
Inside the city
Are the vaults.
Inside the vaults
Are the tunnels and

Inside the tunnels are the trains.
*Inside the trains, hearts,*
Inside the hearts, cities,
*Inside the cities: vaults.*
It is a trap in an exit in a trap.
*It is a treasure stitched within a map.*
And in these lifted cities
*All the windows have been blown out*
Or in these sunken cities
*All the tunnels are filled with dust.*
And it is hard to choose
*Between the two –*
The blown-out open window,
*The sealed-up tube of smoke.*
Running through both
*Like transportation, like clockwork,*
Is a pathway to a vault
*Which may open, or may not.*

*Whenever I hear this song, I think of you, I think: I chose you.*

*But this still won't be enough for you. It would have been better to treat you right, you'll say, than pick you as the single soul to be anointed with my anger. You'll ask that that not be too much to ask. And I know that you're right.*

*But for someone whose tongue was a flower's trumpet of pollen, whose words were extracted by alien insects, and bred into unknown dreams – for someone whose own hands were as hard to feel through as if I was wearing two clay lumps for limbs – I could not have known where to start when it came to tenderness. If I'd ever known, I would have stroked myself into a calmness worthy of being brought and set before you. I would have had something to give you other than my troubled strength.*

I loved you and I was brutal. It's boring and old, I know. But you're clever enough to know all the reasons why a man might put up with the world's woman-hating even though they really loved their wife. We can't be the first two people who have had that conversation. Maybe right now, in a bedroom in Tehran, a man is explaining it to a wife who he's in love with: darling, I can't change the rules we live by.

And I suppose there is a sense in which I hated your knowledge, of languages and of geography, but not your knowledge of any part of love.

It wasn't because I could not accept you had different thoughts to me, but because most of them did not seem like your own. In all those evening conversations, of your great theories and equations that you drew out in the sand, I never felt like I learnt anything about you, like I'd managed to get my hands under your skin. It was like reading a poem through a bad translation. It was like you somehow had another man upon your tongue.

And yes I know that things are hard for women, and I should have been proud of your knowledge, your strength. I really did pay attention when you explained it to me on the beaches. I'd never heard anyone, man or woman, speak the way that you could in those brilliant nights. Aside from the words: your talking was the most supernatural sight I'd seen since I had taken to watching you wash your hair. And I remember what you told me, really: to constantly have to fight to be heard is what makes women seem so shrillish – that women, just as much as men, are neither meek nor suited to permanent combat, either in thought or in sex – that you all had other things scheduled in, before the wars you had to make just to live took over all of your living – that even your strangled call for a ceasefire would be heard as the breaking of peace.

But all you had were these observations. Neither of us had tactics. Even among your army, your team, there are others more suited to *advancing* than you, flat-chested and funny-looking young French girls called Joan, that sort of thing, designed more specifically for things like that. My love, don't waste any more of your precious life fighting that women's lives might not all be wasted. Don't try to level the outside fields. Let's level things in our malleable sand dunes. Let's level things on this bed.

Yes, I don't really know whether any two people can ever truly be one another's equals. But maybe, outside of time, with not much else to do, and with five thousand years between us of watching men and women loving and hurting in their dance, I think we might have a better chance than most. If only we keep our door locked.

That's how we'll access the truth that we need to make us whole again. The secret book of the story of history is of the true loves between men and women when men and women are at war: In a trench in Ypres a young man dreams of resting his head in between his wife's legs again. In a church in oldest Florence, a boy gazes intently at the female holy statue, and uses it to conjure up the curves of his lover's most inner self. Somewhere they are building the first stones of Quebec City in the shape of the bed where a priest used to pray in the kisses between two people still half-asleep.

Even I am not allowed access to this last book. And I don't think they keep it in the room of the library that you are sitting in. Maybe they used it to build the walls, and that's why they're so thick that I can't hear you, and you can't hear me, at your desk three rooms away from mine.

# CAPH

'The proud have digged pits for me, which are not after thy law'

The rift between David and the internationals might have healed, had they not all upped and left, somewhere between the start of settler removals and the Palestinian kidnapping of a blonde English girl. Ricardo sent Anne-Marie a note to say: 'Come with me, I'm going to Rwanda, or maybe the Sudan.' Others embarked for Chechnya; many said they were going to Iraq and some perhaps reached there. But really they could've gone anywhere: that's where they came from after all, and where they were all heading to. They'd been doing this for a while now. The new-exciting-times were dragging on and on. They started young, most of them, cutting their teeth on amateur riots: Genoa, Seattle, low-level overnight-cells everywhere – anti-globalisation protests had taken them all over the world.

And when the new era dawned in that autumn of the new millennium, they all began running, as if touched by a prophecy: away from nothing, and to something – to the centre and fault-line of feelings and lies, to Kabul and Chechnya, or Geneva, Oxford, to places of learning, for ammunition, to each last little refuge of war and the study of it, every last loving enclave of conflict and opposites that was bloody and was sure – and here they held the sounds of bombs as close as babies and they slept with all the local girls. But then, they were young, and the wrong kind of clever, they couldn't be expected to remember too much: they were the sort of people who could sit on trains through Germany and not feel sick or funny. They didn't know the meaning of any kind of terror or war upon it. They couldn't know the meaning of even watching near a war.

And so they ran away again, just as fast as they'd come: away from the inhospitable climates of real sorrow, looking for the transitory place of friendly sufferings, mining precious pieces out of other people's memory lands, and saying what they found and felt was theirs when it was not. Serbia and Somalia and Sierra Leone and Afghanistan and in a series of stinking, over-crowded Parisian suburbs: whichever one had, that summer, been the most aflame. They couldn't stop running when one of them was shot – which happened, from time to time, in these placeless places – because that was what made them run, really, that scent of authenticity, which was strongest during funerals, back home, whipped up to make those who'd stayed there feel all their age and their shame: see how we even have blood amongst us, see how now you can't even touch us. They loved to line up in their suits, and they loved that their suits didn't fit them: a full deck, a legion, a whole armada – the strong ships burdened with manoeuvring this sorrow. Of course they loved to stand there when they looked like that. But then they had to run back to the bedside of the

war, to the late-night war parties, to the joys of borrowed
sorrows, and to the girls like Marla, who between them
they'd probably just dreamt into existence, one day while
sitting on a train. Because they had to buy more time to
stand looking beautiful at future funerals. They ran on and
on.

And then, then, they stopped, finally, and they slept,
finally, hungry – in the airport, in Tel Aviv – where Marie
would see them one last time. They'd be lined up, chewing
on their plastic cups, cutting out pages of the *New Yorker*; as
fraudulent and shot-through as poets in the Spanish Civil
War, and all the other wars that only existed for them to cut
their teeth on. Marie had no opinion of Mahmood Abbas,
but she liked it when he called her international friends 'the
conflict tourists'. They never seemed to see a city or a
country, not really, they just wanted to inhabit a place that
was also an idea: the idea of Palestine, the idea of Harvard,
it didn't matter as long as the name was gold. For all the
horror of their unstructured clothes, they shared the greater
parts of Marie's love of the alpha, the potently symbolic:
they were most at home in the midst, in the stitching, of a
bright national flag with neat lines, in a short and visionary
motto. They had Palestine for the reason, Marie suspected,
that most mothers have their children: to pretend they have
something bigger than themselves that would make it alright
for them to die.

'Take a picture of me with my gun,' a Palestinian boy
would say to them when they walked down the streets
together. The internationals flinched; the Scandinavians
would say something inappropriate in response. The Palestinian boys only thought that they weren't impressed
enough, and ran back into their houses for green bandanas,

kafiyas and bigger guns, or else would run to lurid, cheap-looking posters showing the face of a suicide 'martyr', and pose there awkwardly, as if learning manhood.

All the while, the internationals would watch, already re-writing the scene out in their minds, their emails, and their unreadable, unread blogs, that hid in the darker corners of the internet, like ugly boys at the edge of a school dance. The internationals didn't know how to protest when the Gazans voted for Hamas, and not, say, a group of liberal feminists, or internationals like them. 'It just shows how sad they all are' – like a teenage girl's amateur self-mutilation – that was all the internationals could ever think of to say about this. They had no diplomatic word for what repelled them: perhaps *religiously challenged*. Eventually, during the riots over cartoons – of all things – three of the Scandina-vian volunteers were held at gunpoint by bored kids sent back home from school, and all they thought to cry out was: 'Not Americans! We not Americans!'

The rest of them left in the following months, as Hamas fought with Fatah on the news and in the Gaza streets, on the other side of the enemy. There was something about the queasy-coloured flags that began to fly in victory, which reminded all the internationals of something and they had to get away.

\*

Marie and David sat on the roof, during the day. The schools were running and the children were too busy to come to borrow books from them. Anne-Marie swirled the wine in her glass around mindlessly, and David looked out on to the rooftops of the nearby buildings.

'David . . . maybe we should leave too.'

'Why?' David was impatient, feeling useless that the library wasn't being used, and that there was little else he could do with his day but talk and lie with Marie.

'I just think . . . everyone's leaving.'

'The Palestinians aren't leaving.'

'Well, they are, actually, if they can.'

'Yes but. Not all of them can.' He did a sigh of isn't-that-obvious-to-you.

'Do you get someone out of a well by jumping down into it too?'

'What?'

'I don't know. It's something my grandmother used to say.'

'We're staying, Marie. I'm staying. You do what you want.'

They found their places back in their well-cut silences, as though returning to the part they'd left off in a book. Anne-Marie applied more suntan lotion.

Later in the day, David had to go out to say goodbye to Yoni – one of the first to leave – as he stood in his T-shirt and jeans in the street opposite the library. The sun was in Yoni's eyes, and he squinted as he waved while David walked towards him. He was so still in love with Marla that David knew he hadn't been involved in what was now called 'the pornography incident', and he'd come around for nothing-tasting meals at the library even after the others – to Anne-Marie's relief – had begun to melt away.

Now Yoni said he felt ready to go to Iraq, and that was where he was needed most. He would be collecting information on the many reports of rapes by American soldiers his age or younger. David said he was happy that Yoni was facing his fears and heading back to the American war; Marie thought he was being ridiculous and refused to disguise it. She gave him a quick acknowledgement from the roof as she stood to adjust her bikini. Yoni was wearing his beanie hat and three-day-old stubble, and looked quite good with a rucksack on his back. It was a similar size to the ones Israeli conscripts were forever carting on to Israeli public transport. He was almost as good-looking as a soldier.

The two hugged and patted, patted and hugged: the breadth of their young-man affection. Yoni was the shorter of the two of them, and his trousers lower. He gave David the website details for his travel blog, and David said truthfully that he would try to look it up.

'Be careful,' Yoni said.

'Yeah, you too.'

He turned to go. 'Hey,' Yoni said suddenly. 'A couple of guys are going skiing back in the you-ess this winter. You should totally come along, and bring Marie or whoever, seriously.'

David went back to tell Marie that they'd be staying in the library forever, to prove that they were not like the men and women of all the other nations.

ל

## LAMED
'The wicked have waited for me to destroy me'

But betraying, with beautiful immediacy, all his declarations of forever, it was around this time that David began to visit Mohammad in Geneva.

The war in Iraq had finished its beginnings and begun its long, embarrassing adolescence, and the European winters were dark, despite the snow-shine that greeted David in Switzerland. Mohammad came to meet him at the airport, with flowers as if he was a girl ('You twat, Khan') and a great big stack of international newspapers ('Fuck, yes – I actually started dreaming about the *Economist*').The two spent most of their time in Mohammad's high-ceilinged flat, catching up on the news and the novels that David said that they were supposed to have read by now.

Then they'd walk around the lake together until the evening lazily joined them, and they'd talk about David's plans in Palestine, and the different directions that both the peace process and Mohammad's career could take. The visit was a chance for Mohammad to do all the things in Geneva that he had been too busy or tired to have done by himself. It was never clear to David what Mohammad spent his time doing when he wasn't working: his apartment was clean as an idea, and he didn't seem to know any of his colleagues. David found a neat stack of newspaper clippings about everything that had happened in the West Bank since 2004. David thought perhaps he had to keep on top of that sort of news for his job.

And he soon found that Geneva was Mohammad's apartment writ large. The pavement was so dirtless it was worrying; the homeless asked for change in four languages. Mohammad took David to see the great landmine sculpture, the Red Cross museum and the parts of the building he worked in that were not normally open to visitors.

David said he'd try to come three or four times a year from then on, if his parents still put money into his student bank account, and if there were no problems with him getting from Palestine to Jerusalem airport, and from there on to a flight. His surname always helped him with the last one. On the last night of each visit, David would leave when it was still dark, packing with the light off, trying blindly to write a note to leave on Mohammad's pillow.

*

Once or twice they travelled through Europe, Mohammad carrying both of their bags so David could read the map, without distraction, incorrectly. Travelling was weightless without Marie's make-up-application stops, and they covered ground quickly, exploring Europe's temperate, lesser-loved corners: Ypres, Verdun, The Hague and a weekend in Brussels.

Stopping at memorials only occasionally, they stroked white stone and threw pebbles left on graves between each other, smiling lazily. Pious schoolchildren would titter as the two raced through the sunken fields and the damp-preserved First World War trenches.

The hotels they stayed in were always very quiet. David tried to teach Mohammad to spend the morning in bed, and threatened to pour honey on the keys of his laptop. They spent a Christmas Day in a hotel in Rome, annoying the few sad-eyed staff who'd stayed on with their demands to be humoured and fed, and correcting the Pope's Latin when it wandered out through the radio, being the obnoxious boys they'd secretly missed being, in the more-obnoxious world.

They entered a church in Naples one day to avoid the worst of the heat, so English they had become without Anne-Marie to bully them into either siestas or a feverish project. David had come to visit for two weeks, and they'd taken the train through the Alps to Italy. The church they walked into was for one of the lesser and quite good-looking saints. Mohammad read a tourist guide on the wall as David wiped his forehead by pulling up the bottom of his T-shirt.

With no one in sight but the two of them and an uninterested cleaner, David walked to the font of holy water, pushed his face in, and opened his mouth. Mohammad came up behind him, when he saw what his friend was doing, and then held David steady, as he shook his hair like a dog. Mohammad was smiling at him, mild and water-speckled, but still had one eye out for the church's caretaker.

He thought it was best to pull David gently into one of the wooden pews.

David was gasping but he said felt much better. The heat had been stopping several parts of his head.

'What does it taste like?'

'What?'

'Holy water.'

'I don't know.' David's wet head thought about it. 'Maybe a bit like limes.' He sucked his bottom lip and wiped his face with his T-shirt. Mohammad glanced back at the font, with its trail of copper-green scum that adorned the water-edge of the marble.

'I hope you haven't caught syphilis or something from drinking from that, David.'

*

They went east to Bosnia in the week Mohammad had left of his vacation. He was on an internship for a group that worked on the war crimes tribunals, and spent his time on frighteningly efficient European trains up to The Hague. Mohammad, a good legal student down to his Mohammad-heart, was struck by how under-funded the defence team for the genocide perpetrators was, but he didn't lobby on the issue. He'd long learnt to not look anyone in the eye, which suited his job well. Making their way across Europe, David and Mohammad tried to go to Srebrenica, but no one at Zagreb bus station seemed to understand their pronunciation of it: 'Not exist. Not exist.' They eventually got across the Croatian border on a bus that went from Zagreb to Mostar. The guards pulled out Mohammad at the border check, but it was David's passport that the chain-smoking border men frowned at, as they stroked their dirty thumbs over his first-rate passport photo.

Their first morning in Mostar, they sat in a café drinking Bosnian coffee, and daring each other to jump off the famous bridge that their café-table was giving them their first proper view of. 'You're meant to jump off it if you're in love,' the man in the mosque had told them. Instead the two of them put bets on teenagers and tourists who plunged into the sweet limey river. Mohammad flinched, but only a little, as the boys and men hit the water.

In Sarajevo, David became sick. He vomited his way through four of the daily prayers, as Mohammad sat and stroked his head, and brought bottled water in case the taps had been the cause. Mohammad remembered the other water that his friend had recently drunk of.

David grew paler with the day, and even Mohammad's hand looked strong in his, as they sat or knelt by the cracked toilet bowl. Mohammad had to help David stand and walk from the off-white bathroom to the off-white bedroom, so David could change from his low-slung, sick-smelling trousers and into a pair of shorts. That night, their skin glistening with David's fever and the Eastern European heat, Mohammad looked up at David, into his eyes: a rare act, beautiful and disquieting. David grew paler for a moment and brought his face close enough to Mohammad's that he might read all of its contents. He'd never noticed how Mohammad always tried very hard to smile, so much that he had little lines around his mouth from straining happiness. He wanted to stop him having to try. He wanted to make him happy without effort. The lines that were forming around Mohammad's mouth were saying they were already older than they'd ever meant to be, and David wanted to undo this now with any youthful act that he could grasp at. David was weaker than Mohammad then, but still as he threw his arms around his waist, the force knocked Mohammad on to the hotel bed. And so it was that their kisses fluttered up with the tinkling of the broken pipes, the murmur of the bathroom light, and the South America soap opera that was buzzing down the corridor.

And it was only then that David realised Anne-Marie wasn't the epitome of herself even, and neither would he find it under skirts and sheets in quiet rooms, elsewhere. There was no ideal woman, ideal person: Anne-Marie would be, for him, the little, specific, human root into dreams of all the rest. And nor did other bodies exist to summon up his girlfriend. They were, rather, all of them, wandering versions of the same icon, little particulars of a form unseen – all wearing the veil of Maria's blue dress being lifted over their heads forever and ever.

\*

Mohammad, flinching from the window-sunshine, went down to the hotel lobby barefoot, feeling the coolness of tiles and the heat of the sun together. He told the old woman at the front desk, Mohammad-quietly, that they'd be staying for longer than they'd thought. The woman smiled. Her face did clever things when she smiled, and for a moment she was not old. She gave him a small cup of bitter Bosnian coffee, and told him about how her husband had had to climb through a pitch black tunnel, water up to his waist, during the war, to reach her and bring her food. Mohammad re-told David the story when he came up to the bedroom, and the two of them smiled at the thought of it.

Then they both felt terrible for smiling, so they talked seriously about the Bosnian war, and the books they'd read about it.

When they didn't leave the hotel for two days, the same woman knocked on their door and called out in her accent: 'I hope you are not dead. I have left you something.' Mohammad went out and saw that the whole floor outside of their neglected door was covered in rich Bosnian cakes and halva wrapped in brown paper. It took him three trips to carry them back to the bed to David. And so they lay there for another day, pastry-fuelled, reading the international editions of the papers, and listening to the first Franz Ferdinand album on the laptop that David had bought in Brussels. David had recovered from his sickness, and Mohammad looked healthier than anyone had ever seen him, although he still had the UN-sponsored bags under his eyes, from not sleeping properly. He wondered how David had got so practised at being awake through the night, because it wasn't the same tiredness that writing essays or Geneva reports had brought him.

They turned on the tiny, tinny television that night, expecting *Friends* dubbed into Serbo-Croat, or another South American melodrama. But they were met instead with the face of the professor. He was mid-sentence; he looked smart and clean-shaven – his face and thoughts suited television, reassured people that things were clear and simple. He was one of panel of critics and analysts on a British debate programme.

The woman presenting the programme was stopping him mid-sentence, asking him to clarify what he meant. 'Aren't you essentially saying that you condone suicide-bombers?'

'You misunderstand, of course there's a difference between sanctioning murder . . .'

'So you agree that it is murder . . .'

'Between that and saying that you *can* understand how desperate Palestinian lives are as a result of Zionist imperial fascism.' He tapped the expensive-looking studio table with his palm in time with his words.

Mohammad raised his eyebrows. This wasn't the blood-less language he'd become used to in Geneva, and he could hardly stomach meat since Bosnia. David was nodding along to the glow of the screen. 'They always try to make anyone who disagrees with Israel sound like a terrorist.'

'Yes. I suppose that's not very helpful,' Mohammad looked uncomfortable as he pulled his jumper over a T-shirt that he'd had to borrow from David. 'But, I mean . . . the problem is – some people who disagree with Israel are terrorists, so you have to be clear, that, you know . . .' Mohammad wasn't sure how to finish. He hated these sorts of conversations, and was never sure how they'd begun.

David spoke evenly, facing the screen: 'I think the real tragedy is that these people have so absolutely nothing to live for, that they'd go and blow themselves up.'

And Mohammad didn't want to argue with his friend, so said: 'I guess we have to have empathy with every side of it,' and took out the American newspaper that had cost him 30 Bosnian KM. David leaned over to kiss the lowered eyelids as he read.

\*

They both loved Sarajevo: they had empathy with every side of it. They spent hours in the Turkish quarter, feeling tall next to the tiny shop-fronts, like real people in a doll's house, though David said that was a colonialist thing to say, and then they felt English-guilty. They'd walk along the river bank and kiss by the famous and the not-famous bridges. It didn't occur to them that it might offend people, make them feel confused and funny. Sarajevo was so quiet now anyway: they had whole streets to themselves. Mohammad even took the lead in deciding they should go to one of the old Croatian churches, and it was so deserted inside that they could've done anything.

And so it was that all the days they spent together in Sarajevo were quietly, timidly perfect. But it was the evenings, most of all, that pinned them down to love: the smell and shape of Sarajevo evenings were a dialect they quickly learnt, unobviously different from the languages that it lived beside. Before the Sarajevo nights, and after Sarajevo days, was a gap to be rested in – to drink from fountains, or take your boots off – either in the blue of Virgin Mary statues, or else in the blue of Turkish glass. It opened its gates, the evening, and did not check its borders closely, let in clumsily – the tourists – the soldiers – the elderly – and most of all the women – in their red and blue dresses, like meaningless flags of forgotten places now. And then a banquet of dusk-smells, a market of ink-shades, would try to forge an independent country, would try to carve out a brief breath, a yawn-stretch, between the gathering forces on the hilltops – the armoured shapes of dark and light – that laid siege to these Sarajevo evenings, during the nights and the days.

*

And then, during a Sarajevo-perfect day, they went and found the perfect croissant. It was a mathematical probability that, somewhere, proportionally perfect pastries were being consistently turned out every morning from mathematically miraculous ovens. But no one else seemed to know or notice, as though everyone had forgotten that year's pilgrimage to this heavenly place, this spring of visions. It was in the third street from the mosque with the clock, in the Turkish quarter, and if you ever meet Mohammad he won't mind drawing you a map.

They'd found it walking through an evening that they had just found the key to: not walk too quickly, not talk too much. Mohammad marvelled at the rows of crescents, didn't know which one to pick. David smiled his most alpha and everything smile at them and said: 'Come on, let's go in. I've been waiting so long to find a place like this.'

Inside the café, an old man with a face for Italian currency stood behind a counter. The gold-baked perfections glistened in his face like pirate gold. 'Dobar dan.' David smiled and pointed at the pastries behind the counter, and his finger found itself pleasantly up against the coolness of the glass.

'Dva . . . no, tri . . . no, cetiri . . . hvala mnogo.' He had learnt enough Bosnian to be greedy, but still remembered how to say thank you ('Hvala mnogo,' he would say silently to him every evening, in the dialect). He carried the four croissants back to Mohammad. Shyly, Mohammad borrowed David's smile.

And from that day on David went out every morning to buy their perfect breakfast from the old man who looked gold. He brought some extra back each day to thank the woman who ran the hotel for her earlier generosity. The sun shone and they all ate sugared things. Everything was kindness and delicious. Lying on the bed, Mohammad could easily have grown as chunky as Gauguin's Mary in Tahiti, for David wouldn't let him even try to get out of bed without putting three perfect croissants in his mouth. They curled up together on the bed like the symbol of an almost-eclipsed moon.

They shared themselves between Sarajevo and the hotel. They shared the hotel time between kisses and whispers.

'Have you ever loved another man?'

'Daniel Deronda.'

'I'm being serious.'

There was no part of Mohammad's forehead that David hadn't kissed while asking him these sorts of questions: how many others? no others? what did aloneness feel like in the night? Mohammad never asked these things of David. One perfect morning David took his hand and said: 'I'm sorry that you weren't the first.' Mohammad looked down at the held hand. 'I don't mean Marie . . . the professor and I . . . I'm sorry.' Mohammad offered him the last croissant, because David really did look sorry. He watched him as he ate. Then David lay on top of him, slightly higher, the top of one's hips at the bottom of the other's, so that Mohammad might kiss his stretched Adam's apple. The two could have lived side by side for two thousand years and never flare up into so much as a heated word. They had found the perfect crescent. David could have spent fifty years running his fingers over Mohammad's sleeping lips. And there was so much of the world still to be sorted out between their two clever loving heads.

'See, whenever people talk about whether Muslims can "ever" be true Europeans, they forget – there always, always *have* been Muslim Europeans – there have always been Bosnians.' David said, talking like the professor, as they lay there in the night, shining with lingering and mixed perspiration, each trying to read the newspaper.

'Yes, I suppose. Although it's not really the point that they should treat Muslims better because they're "really" Europeans too. They should just do it because, it's, well . . .' he searched through the terminology that Geneva had quickly coached him in '. . . nice. Because it's a right thing to do.' He shrugged his shoulders to say sorry-I-can't-phrase-it-better. David smiled and entangled their legs further.

'Yeah, you're right. I know you're right. But it's a good point to make to people who care about that kind of thing, you know: beat them on their own terms.'

Mohammad nodded and closed his eyes. They were both too tired to try to change any more of the world before they slept. David reached his arms around to Mohammad's back so he could feel his favourite part, just under the shoulder blades.

David asked him later that night: 'Do you feel at home here? In a Muslim country, I mean?'

'Well.' Mohammad shifted. 'I don't know.'

'I just mean, you know, *ummah* and everything . . .'

'Well.' He rubbed his hand on the back of his own head as he now more usually did on David's. 'I'm an only child.' He shrugged his shoulders.

'I don't know what you mean.'

'I don't know, David.' He turned so they were facing the same direction, and put his arms though David's armpits so he could stroke his chest and stomach. 'I find it hard to think of anyone as my brother.'

# RUMI

The angel-devils of the untried men led me through all their old homelands, pointing out a lesser-loved passage between two mountains, or stroking me shyly towards the promise of a lake. All across Khorasan and to Baghdad, and for many months, the untried men who watched over the earth then paid special attention to me, stood gently on each of my shoulders, as the rolls of my scrolls nestled against my side, like a wife or like a gun.

More of the letters between Samson and Delilah arrived: their imperfect poetry and their human love – and it was funny, in the way something could be funny now, that all the while I'd been writing of God, and my poems were taken as words of human love, so they'd been trying to write out their love, and it had got mixed up in a God-story. I wondered how and if these elements could become untangled, or if that wouldn't be a bit like trying to untangle veins from a body they ran through. So I continued to follow them, the angel-devils and the love-letters, hoping they'd come to lead me to a peace-land, or a mouth to the cave of caves. The letters came at night, like thieves, curled up inside Psalm 119, which curled in on itself on my side, as I curled up on myself in tiredness, and as my country collapsed in on itself.

But if I ignored a whispered message from the angel-devils of the untried men – if I was stubborn, or if winds wouldn't blow in from the island where they lived now – I'd make a wrong turning, and Delilah's and Samson's letters wouldn't reach me any more. I unrolled the Psalm those mornings, and it was barren as a harvest in the war-time. They would only lead me if I followed them. So I learnt to listen more carefully to the guiding voice of the untried men, as unsure as I was – as the whole world was – of whether they were right.

It took Toghril Beg fifteen years to walk to Baghdad. The great leader of those I lived under in Konya, I kept thinking of him walking and walking. For fifteen years. To stop being a shepherd and start looking like a prince: which is why he took so long. He was doing what we all did. The young leadership of the Seljuks, still scrappy, amateur pillagers, divided their leadership, headed east and west. Toghril set off as a Turcoman but arrived as a classical Arab leader, clean and built precisely to rule them. He spent fifteen years in walking, drawing to him, or trying to, Arabs as ballast, culture to barter with, customs as a weapon. Even when he finally arrived, the Caliph wouldn't deign to meet him for three years.

But everything came to meet me, before I was even there: all the specifics of horrors rushed into my face. I smelt Baghdad on the horizon for weeks, and it was the smell of poetry: I approached timidly in awe of its powers. Because you'd be wrong to think of weakness, though the children looked weak as they ran crying in all directions, though the trees looked weak as they burnt or leant in broken shame, and though the women visibly cursed their weakness in running, as their skirts held back the powers of their legs. But that was the poetry of Baghdad, the very strength of the horror of it. The strength of smells, the strength of noise, the strength of death, the strength of colour: that is what I mean by poetry.

I'd thought the scales to measure horror had been destroyed in Kabul. God humbled me once more, and that was the poetry of Baghdad. The horror of the greatness of God, the explosiveness of the particulars – that even when you think you've seen the worst thing, the most explosive thing, that still God surprises you in every burning instant. That is what I mean by poetry.

I didn't sleep, after coming to Baghdad, because it could not be a place for sleeping, now and perhaps forever. Still I left the scrolls untouched at night, not watching, not wishing to curse anything, and more letters arrived, like greetings, a cruel joke of greetings: tales of love in a time of war. I tried to imagine where they were, where exactly, in what sphere, Samson and Delilah lay. I began to wonder what they needed me for, how I was involved in this. In his letters, Samson spoke of a library. I asked them to guide me to a library.

The angel-devils did their best, limited in movement as they were, on their island now. In secret breezes, burnt with tears, they led me to the library least likely at that moment to be a source of life and nourishment. The large white curving building, like a religious hat, like a pot for precious ointments, I thought I was perhaps just dreaming of this library – the way that starving men conjure up their dreams of food. I only believed in the library for real when I saw the blood upon the floor, and the dying fires in the corners. It had been ransacked: by the people who came here, by the people who lived here, by those who should and who should not be here – no one was exempt from their part in this. Like the Mongols my father had tried to spare us from, all those centuries ago – here they were – caught up with me finally, burning civilisations, an offering for nobody in a poetry of horrors.

I stood in another library, then, feeling as though all doors in my life only led into other libraries, burning books, that the doors on my life's choices were covers of books, and burning contents.

I hated them then. Not the invading Mongols, not the pillaging thieves, not the zealots or the heretics or any of these. I hated Samson and Delilah for tangling me up with their story, like some sick God had picked up two books, and spread their pages, pushed them into one another, a mutant coupling, the beast with two book-spines. Why had they woken from their place in the pages? Why now try to re-write their ending? I've watched, from time to time, most modern people resurrect an old, forgotten myth as a blunt tool to explain their new world with, trying it on again like a rediscovered dress. But the myth isn't what you need in the horrors of the new world: the myth is the worm in the truth. If only there was a recurring myth to remind them of this too. I travelled through Serbia in my caravan once too; I know what a myth and a poem can do. I cried, in the library, and was ashamed of crying, not for the people and the burning in Baghdad – which my tears could never ease – but to the two old lovers: what did they want? What did they want? I felt like a child between warring parents: what can you possibly want from me?

I opened the scrolls in anger: angry at the filth, the obsession, the bad poetry, of love of all things, that they'd carelessly brought me into, and in a time of war.

But instead of a letter from Samson or Delilah, instead of any of their love and hatefulness – or what, to me, then, was hateful – curled up inside the Psalm was a story about a woman and a man, living in a library. Living in the times I was almost living in, after the planes and the new pilgrims. Something I could prevent: somewhere where I could act, and wipe the helplessness of Baghdad horrors from me, get its smell out of my nose. The angel-devils led me out of Baghdad – the shame of leaving and the shame of staying being the same, being an equal horror, for all of us who weren't from Baghdad then. The untried men led me, starving, shocked, towards Jerusalem – like a star whose existence has been disproved by laws, the untried men would guide me.

# MEM

'How sweet are thy words unto my taste!
Yea, sweeter than honey to my mouth'

Because all Western women are whores, or because the heat nearly killed her, Marie bought a bright pink inflatable paddling pool and set it up on the roof of the library. She'd had some trouble getting the thing past the security checks. A spotty, unsure soldier had made her open up the box that the pool had been packaged in at the Jerusalem super-market. She had a vision of the boy shooting his bullets through it to stop it from making her happy. But he just smirked, acted confident, and inspected the contents. And now it was hers: the thought of it warmed her all the way up the stairs.

David was in Europe with Mohammad. Anne-Marie didn't even pretend to attend to the daily duties of the library while he was away. The Palestinian girls just let them-selves in now, but they rarely came anyway when Justin Timberlake was on tour.

She took the box straight up to the roof, and she got down on her knees for it. It probably took ten minutes or more for her to inflate the paddling pool, but to Marie it was but a light-headed blur of dreamy possibilities. For someone who could never bring herself to buy a sex toy because they were so often this shade and feel of plastic, Marie was charmingly charmed by the translucent pink and the gaudy prints of tropical fish that were swimming suspended in the fuchsia. She carried seven buckets of precious Palestinian water up the ladder to the roof uncomplainingly. No one who knew her would have believed it, had they seen her then.

She stripped evenly to her bikini in front of the midday Middle Eastern sun. The sky was the light blue shade of redemption, and the skyline was quiet as grace. She knelt inside the pink and rubbed handfuls of water on to her limbs, preparing, then leant back slowly into the cool. Everywhere it touched her she turned to gold, or faint water-speckles and goose pimples. Her hands facing heavenward, her hair awash with light, and with the reflections of the printed tropical-fish, Anne-Marie breathed as slowly as the sweetness of death, and her breasts rose and fell again glacially, out of the bright shallow pool. She knew that she would have been the first thing seen by any aerial sniper.

But if there really was a link, of praying and of geography, which shuttled its own pricy spiritual ferry-service, from Jerusalem up to the stars, its holy portal was to be this oval, the heart of Marie's pink bath – and her halo of gold hair, and Versace bikini – to be the only lightness that was set down there to guide us.

Sweet Maria: blue and pink as sky and water, almost naked, bathed in dreaming breath. Oh God, is what she vaguely thought at the cool of it, as she faced forward, unflinchingly, at Palestine's watching sky. Then she closed her eyes and moved her legs together and apart: the cool water that rocked between her legs was icy and different kinds of divine, it washed over her in rhythms that she could only half control. She remembered this from being a girl on the beach in southern France in her summers, when she'd consciously try to not fight the current of the sea. She felt like she was being studied, benignly, and there were no need for displays from her now, the water would be the veils she made and remade for cleverness, for men.

And though the great epic of pretending would resume, she knew, now, it was beyond her choosing – knew most of all in these pauses from lies – it would still happen, when women were equal, it would still happen, when the countries were free. She refused the universal alibi of things not being right in these times: her pretending, her pretence, was hers and her fault alone. Her ears filled with the paddling-pool water, and this was God now trying to tell her – you are all just so much noise Anna-Maria, the times you live in aren't your excuses. Under the water, Marie understood for once, and she knew, for once, in her little breath of clarity here, that she should write it down, photograph it, or scrawl it in gunpowder while she still had the chance, before she slipped back under into pretending, mindless pretending, daydreaming abstractly about herself from the point of view of men. She knew she should capture it, for later unwrapping in pretending-times, something real-smelling to bring her back from all the vagueness, but lying there it felt like her hands had already turned themselves into gold or clay.

In her secret clarity she saw and felt the presence. And if the glory of God was a dream into which we would wake,

Marie leant into it, moist and sleepy, half-awake. My soul melteth for heaviness, her shifting legs sang as they moved in the water, and the law of thy mouth is better unto me than the thousands of gold and silver. She opened her legs and the pool's water leapt to the sides, on to the concrete and her sunglasses. Quicken thou me according to thy word, for I am become like a bottle in the smoke. She arched her back and pointed her toes. I have seen an end of all perfection; but thy commandment is exceeding broad. I opened my mouth, and panted: for I longed for thy commandments. She moved her legs together again, and the water burst forth in every direction. She sang to herself the centre of the psalm: How sweet are thy words unto my taste – yes, sweeter than honey to my mouth.

*Dear Samson,*
*I found this in the library and I thought of you. It is a bookmark:*

> *on nights like these*
> *by heavy desks*
> *for those alone and*
> *worn as sea-trunks*
> *moths of pages*
> *left in margins*
> *petals of letters*
> *loving as needlepoint*
> *for he who conjures*
> *loving as needlepoint*
> *petals of letters*
> *left in margins*
> *moths of pages*
> *worn as sea-trunks*
> *for those alone and*
> *by heavy desks*
> *on nights like these*

*I think it is clever and not true at all. That's why it made me think of you. You wrote that you wanted to give me back my body. I know all men who are true lovers have always dreamt of this. Casanovas, little librarians, carefully searching in the coyly spread books: where did she leave her lesser smiles, her uneven breathing and the girlish turning inwards of her feet, that she still does sometimes, but only when no one is watching?*

*I suppose that this is a way of loving, in the silent compiling of footnotes.*

*But even the man who wants to steal you back from the world is a kind of a thief. Even if he wants to be the pool for your smiling reflection, the sky for beauty to circle in, as Rumi says, and to teach you (for the man knows better) how to love yourself – still try to remember that women already have enough mirrors, for the most part. And rather than learning to love themselves, they just break them when they're unhappy.*

*Oh Samson, I know what I'm doing now. This is only the second letter in forever and already I'm pushing, pushing you, pushing everything: as far as I possibly can. Finding the faults of even the way that you love and the way you are giving. And I'm sorry.*

*I guess we're both still trying to conquer each other. Every country wants to see how many acres of land they get away with claiming. It's awful to think of us like that, isn't it? You and I, who were once as peaceful as bees. I want to reclaim you from the world as well. I want to make you my own Samson again.*

*Be only for me. That's all I ask. I'll be all you need. I'll make you clean. With your head in my lap or by a river, I will wash you, just the way that I used to, or clean you and save you with a jar of oil, like Romans do, and with even greater force. Let me pick off every itchy little Wagner and score-writer, and kiss all the shades of* your skin spotless of the clingy dreams of acne-ridden Israeli boy soldiers.

Did you know that they named a combat unit after you, in 1948? Did it reach you, in your room of the library? Like you wrote in your letter, these were the times of the living paradigm. Somebody thought it would be appropriate then.

Your name was in the headlines again – the Samson Foxes, they were called. It zapped me like an electric fly-trap, even all the way here where I was, the way a child buzzes automatically when they overhear the word 'sex'.

The Samson Foxes. Take us the foxes, the little foxes, that spoil the vines: for our vines have tender grapes. So the Song of Songs says. But then grapes make themselves tender only when they are ready for eating. And during that time, many women travelled to Jerusalem to find them, to find my Samson or to find anyone – you know how oversexed the quietest people get at the mention of war. I watched the ready girls and women from the quiet of my roof, as they all filed their nails especially, and bristled as their fake Dior dresses wilted like flowers in the heat.

I'm not jealous of these girls. But nor are they my handmaidens, or my bitchy little cheerleader companions. I have no female friends, and everybody knows by now anyway that the sisterhood is a lie. But in our paper house of love they are the more impotent spies.

I think they thought I was their guide, in 1948 and forever. And I've heard that other female figures have been proud when they see their mirror-versions echo down through convent dormitories, and down through the pages of the better kind of magazines that have pictures of women in them. But I'm not interested in them. Mainly because they are not you. And also because I don't believe in using other lives, other whole lives, as a means of brightening our fireworks. I do not want the wedding gift of thirty virgins shipwrecked. People forget that I too am a girl reduced to decorating the side of a book's margin. Let everyone at least be the main character in their own brief, boring narrative. Let there be no female Choruses. Let there be no messengers. Let there be no Messengers.

So many women have thought that I was their guide: I was more following than followed. And I have sat still at this desk for the longest part of all my time. The women sang in the round the hymn of the myth-hunters – dreaming of you, dedicated to me – as they sniffed out anything, down Jaffa Road:

The world is full of copies of 'Le Monde'
*Always slightly out-of-date*
They fill the lobby of my sad hotel
*And I look upon them with a weary recognition.*

Always slightly out-of-date
*I still go dancing with the would-be soldiers*
And I look upon them with a weary recognition
*The walk back is as long as two or as one.*

I still go dancing with the would-be soldiers:
*I am tired as a library*
The walk back is as long, as two, or as one.
*To think I used to dream about the whole army*

I am tired as a library.
*The world is full of copies of 'Le Monde'.*
To think I used to dream about the whole army:
*They fill the lobby of my sad hotel.*

*I am tired of everything that is not you. Give yourself to me again, and completely: tell me all of your secrets. Let me be the only one who knows how you are weak. And make them take all of their tanks off the lawn of my grief.*

נ

# NUN
'I am afflicted very much: quicken me,
O Lord, according to thy word'

An email came from Mohammad one spring morning as
Marie sat at the library's desk, with the new computer that
David had bought on his most recent trip to Europe:

*'Hello David.*
*I'm coming to Israel. I hope that that's good news, and that you
don't mind that it is Israel, and not Palestine. Now that my internship is over, I've had to find another organisation to work for, to get
more experience before going into the job directly 'above me', as it
were, in Geneva. So I've found a human rights advocacy group in
Tel Aviv that does a lot of stuff on women's rights – which was
kind of my thing in Geneva for the last six months – and they work
in affiliation with Amnesty International, so tick all the right
boxes, really. I don't start straight away, but there are some seminars I'd like to go to at Tel Aviv University, which my old boss*

*wrote me a reference to get on – so, fingers crossed, I should be there in about four weeks.*

*Write back if you can. I know the connection is tricky where you are.*

*Love from Mohammad.'*

Connections were always tricky, but still not insurmountable. Marie and David went to visit him first thing, arguing on the bus all the way over, and arriving at Mohammad's apartment almost before he'd arrived there himself. They helped to carry his suitcases up to his apartment. Mohammad cooked for them, and they drank a disgusting kind of kosher wine, which Mohammad had accidentally bought at the late-night corner shop. Mohammad told them about his job and developments in women's legal rights in the Middle East. Even Anne-Marie paid attention, so much had she missed her friend.

They spent the evening standing on Mohammad's small balcony, in a row and a little drunk, their glasses in their hands, dangling over the edge. For each, it was their first experience of Tel Aviv, and all were a little enchanted – David despite himself, Mohammad in his even-handedness, Marie in the kind of unalloyed awe that made her squeeze things and hands and herself in ways that hurt the others.

Mohammad said the airport was very beautiful; it reminded him of the UN buildings. It even had a fountain on the ceiling, Tel Aviv defying the possible from the first moment. They all liked the way that people here wrote their graffiti out in the three languages, English, Arabic and Hebrew, one under the other, like an Adidas stripe. Stencil graffiti had replaced tagged and scrawled vandalism across the world by now, which suited boxy Hebrew letters more than any other language. The walls were all covered in painted words and the meaningless sprayed residue that is found at the edge of stencils.

And Marie was in heaven here, perfectly balanced, bathed temperately in the city heat and the cool of her blue dress. In less than twenty-four hours, she gave herself to Tel Aviv. She saw an image of herself in the hardened, happy young, who she watched playing volley-ball on the beach into the evening, lit by the joy of their illegal beach fires. How could these people be David's enemy? They even danced in the traffic.

She went back on to the balcony when David and Mohammad were asleep. David had said an awkward goodbye to Mohammad, after Marie had made Mohammad awkward in turn with hugging him goodnight so tightly. Then in their too-clean, undecorated, bedroom for the night, David had held Marie's body close as if to stop her defecting. They struggled to keep quiet for Mohammad's sake, and bit each other's shoulders to silence themselves. Now David slept undressed and with a frown upon his face.

And on the balcony, Marie watched a party in a house down the street, at which, in another world, she was capturing some happy room, spinning drunk, with a student who knew Spanish and wanted to show her a new way to dance that ended up with them falling and laughing. She traced out various lives she could have had if she hadn't come to Palestine with David, different men and boys and parties, perhaps even different thoughts. From where she stood, high-up and alone, she listened to the clinking and breaking of glasses, the giggles and screams, the endless youthful conversations. She listened to Tel Aviv: she who never listened to anyone.

Everything about the city was alpha, human-perfect, even the way that the streets were full of cats, stray cats, and all smelt of it. Everything was ripe, the Parisian-seeming rudeness was the opposite of the stale contempt of London, and even the cheap, rotten shop-fronts and the stenches were references only to themselves: nowhere else did what they did, and did it in Hebrew. The old tongue seemed to hardly believe that it had been resurrected by the modern, dirty, happy young, and it leapt from taxi to palm tree to sidewalk as unsure as Samson of its own new strength.

Though Anne-Marie had always been phobic, girlishly, of the cities in a country that weren't the capital, or else an idea somehow, like Oxford, she knew now that Tel Aviv was to be a great star in her private constellation. Like the capital city of glory: either hauled from the shore by Modernist angels, or else born of the most mutated kind of coral. The Bauhaus buildings curved for her to lean toward them. And Tel Aviv loved Anne-Marie fiercely then, through all its shards of champagne-glass shrapnel, from Mike's Place to the chunky Jaffa edges, from the nightly car-crashes to the sickly stray cats, caught the light and sang out to her that night, on the balcony, sang to her and to Israel and to all the Israel past-lives, through the arms of the civilians, through the legs of all the strong girls: *Do not live forever in your darkest hour – build your city on your joy.*

\*

But David wouldn't go to Israel again. He stored up his rage until they'd finished eating in their kitchen back in the rooms above the library. Marie hadn't been suspecting it, hadn't dressed accordingly, or sharpened all her words.

'I don't know what's happened to Mohammad.'

'What's happened to Mohammad?'

'Living next to those fucking monsters.'

'Leave him alone. He probably chose here because then he could be close to us.'

'Why do you say that?' He bristled like heat.

'Jesus Christ, I don't know. I just don't think it's a crime to live in Tel Aviv.'

'People support the crimes of others in every choice they make, even if they don't choose it.'

'That doesn't even make sense as a sentence.'

Perhaps he hadn't prepared for his rage, either.

'Oh, I'm so sorry Marie,' he had rolled up his sleeves, 'it's just – some of us have *jobs* to do.'

That night, as he lay on the bed, Marie came over, finished brushing her hair, and pawed at his chest while he lay scowling, reading an Arabic newspaper slowly as a child. So rare – in all history; in all images – for him to be the one lying there, his lips curled like the ends of scrolls, and she wanting to undo him. He didn't stop reading his newspaper and she sat down on the bed. She took off her peach dressing-gown. He didn't stop frowning, but one arm reached instinctively for the lowest part of her back, and drew her to him. He stayed on his back. Marie watched him very closely as they moved together, their faces not matching their acts. David looked so strange to her that it almost stopped him from being beautiful. She didn't know how to pull away after they'd finished, and he wouldn't shift his legs to help, so she stayed, sitting with her back arched, until he fell asleep. Only then could she put her arms around him, and let sleep in turn fumble over her.

\*

And so it was that, from that night, David's mood was like his ruffled hair that, in Palestine, had been too long out of place to ever be pup-licked back to its original calmness. He was all full of decrees and judgements, the likes of which had already wormed their way between him and the departed internationals. He said he wanted to run his library, and be able to look in the eyes of the Palestinians. This desire wormed its way between his heart and Marie.

He still used all his left-over energy on her every night he could, and she still watched, smiling, as the schoolgirls, skipping or turned back from school, struggled with each other to be beside him. And they still argued as quickly as they used to – *you think you're the Messiah; you're not as sweet as you think; no one likes armed missionaries; think about who you sound like* – but despite these happy constants of their old life together, things were beginning to change. He wouldn't walk around the streets with her any more, and refused to have days-off on the beach; he never took her to the part of the wall that Banksy had painted, like he'd promised, and he no longer laughed when she taught the schoolgirls lines from crude American hip-hop. It was no longer charming to see her drinking wine, all bubble-bathed, after his days of death and ambulances. It was no longer adorable how she killed bugs with squirts of the perfume that he'd been forced to bring her back from Europe.

The Israelis imposed a curfew on the village after a suicide bomb and a too-eager celebration at the martyr/killer's funeral, which David stood on the edge of to photograph, and which Marie had watched alone from the roof.

During the quiet, shaking nights of the curfew, fragile like the skin that grows on water, David heard Marie's laugh, beautiful laugh, flying up from where she sat reading and he flinched. And it was a terrible thing, to flinch at her happiness, but he would've done anything to stop her laughing in what was supposed to be the dignity of silence now.

Then two evenings after the curfew started, as David uploaded his photos on to his laptop, he heard Anne-Marie stamping unevenly between the bathroom and the bed. She came to the top of the stairs in her socks, Dior cardigan and two pairs of overlapping underwear, reinforcing opaqueness. She was whimpering and her hair was tied in plaits, the way it was when she felt sick.

'David, I don't know what to do. I . . . I don't know what to do.' She was crying little tears and her chin shook. He came to the bottom of the stairs: still such a distance.

'What's wrong? I'm working.'

'I've run out of tampons. I feel all sore and horrible. David, will you run out and get me some?'

He looked at his watch.

'Annie, the curfew's started.'

'Can't you drive to Jerusalem for me? It really, really hurts – I need paracetamol as well.' She made a funny face like an old French clown: she'd never mastered sadness.

David lifted the front of his T-shirt to wipe his sweating face. He sat at the bottom of the stairs: still such a distance.

'What do Palestinian women do when they can't get tampons?'

'How the bloody hell should I know. *Please* drive to Jerusalem, David. It's a really heavy blood flow, it's ruining my clothes. And it hurts.'

'Well, can't the girls here help you? Can't you ask them

what they do? What do you talk about with them all day?'

*You. You you you you you you you you. And they will love this story.*

'I don't know, stupid things, not things like this. David, please, please . . .'

'I'm sorry Marie, no more exceptions. If they can cope, so can you.'

'You fucking bastard.' She stomped off, slightly bent over, back to their bedroom.

'You're behaving like a child,' he called after her.

More days spent in the bathtub.

\*

And so there are various versions to the history of his betrayal: either assault or withdrawal, either the achingly slow months of souring or the sudden blow of his misjudged act. Afterwards she realised one set fire to the other somehow – a year earlier David wouldn't have done what he did on their last day, and so it was that the origins of conflicts would always be untraceable for them.

The assault could have been predicted, if it had been thought about. David wanted so badly to prove that he was not like the internationals who had fled – make a final sign that he'd made a choice, that he was a grown man, that he'd stick here with Palestine – that one night he let a man commonly known to be a militant hide in their library for the night. In the morning, as Marie came down the stairs in her soft dressing gown, the man screamed where he lay, under their blankets in the corner of the library – a cry that sounded girlish somehow, a cry only for himself. Anne-Marie chased him out the front door, shaking and screaming in her Arabic, threatening to tell the Israelis. Those few who had not already heard her fury fly all across Jerusalem.

David woke and came out of the bedroom just in time to hear the bathroom door slam. He knocked and spoke through the door for almost an hour, leaning his back against the unsanded wood, first to be tender and appeal to her better nature, and then because he really needed the toilet.

Eventually he went out to the alley to piss. He heard the bathroom door creak open and Marie's pounding footsteps around the stunned, aching library.

He went up to find her on the roof. She was wearing her Versace bikini in the paddling pool. She had stolen his aviator sunglasses relatively recently. She frowned in the sun like the soldiers did.

'You're not a child any more, Maria,' he said in a voice of threatening calm.

'Glad you noticed,' she said, obnoxiously placing her hand on her hip, to say: look at this.

'You can't behave like this, it's a fucking war zone . . .'

'I *know* it's a war zone, David, that's why I don't think it's a particularly genius plan to invite around members of Hamas.'

'They would have killed him if they found him.'

'They would have fucking killed us if they'd found him in our house!'

'That's what everyone else said – that's why he had nowhere.'

'No. No. No no-room-at-the-inn crap. You're not the victims. He's a bastard. You're a bastard. You should all just . . . fuck off.' David's calmness was always the rudest, cruellest response to one of her rages. She threw the sunglasses at him.

'Why are we here if we can't actually help people?' he asked. He picked up the sunglasses and put them on.

She stood up suddenly. Water followed and exploded over both of them.

'Why are we here, David?'

'What?'

'Seriously. Is this why you came here? To help a bunch of fanatics who blow themselves up on buses, who think that people who don't believe in Allah should have their heads cut off, who attack Israeli women – attack *Palestinian* women, half the time, from what Mohammad told me – for what? Is that why we're here?'

'Because people need us here. Nobody cares about them, they're just left to . . .'

'They need *us*, do they? Specifically?'

'They need me.'

Marie nodded her head and smiled viciously. 'Yes dear, of course they do. How could they not? You're the full-stop at the end of the word "Cohen".' This was a good line, she thought. 'You're the whole fucking *line* and *edifice* of the Brahmin caste. God forbid anyone but you could save them.'

'Don't enjoy this. It's not some game.'

'Yeah, I haven't had this much fun since Ramadan.'

David let out a great cry of fury, finally. '*You* are just *incapable* of thinking beyond *yourself*! You think no one else has a *soul*. You don't open up to them, you don't *let* them like you . . .'

'Whereas you . . .'

'Whereas I *try* to connect with the people here, because

they deserve to be treated with a bit of fucking respect. Because they deserve *honesty* and *understanding* from us, if we're . . .'

'Why do you pretend not to be Jewish, then?'

'What?'

'If they deserve honesty. Why don't you ever tell them you're Jewish?'

'Don't you *dare* define me, it is *not* your place to try to . . . to – don't you ever tell me what I am.' He threw the paddling pool over in fury. The water soaked only his shoes, not her bare feet.

'Yes, because it's all about your clever ideas of identity, and nothing to do with the fact that half of them are anti-Semites, who . . .'

'After what they've been through . . .'

'*After what they've been through,*' she mimicked through her bitter accent. Although she knew he never would, right then he looked as if he was about to hit her.

He stormed down from the roof. Now it was his turn to lock himself in the bathroom. He listened at the door as Marie knocked over book-piles and bookshelves, and the 1920s windows shuddered, nervous. He heard her running up the stairs, and trying the bathroom door. When it didn't open, she shouted, 'Fine! That's just fine!' into the wood of the door frame. He heard her run down the stairs again. He heard the front door open and then slam.

He opened the bathroom window, and saw her little figure burning its way down the dusty street, the way that his Arabic name from the schoolgirls had danced in the fire, from one end to the other. He leant out of the window.

'So long, Marianne!'

'Oh fuck off, David!'

PART THREE

# SAMECH

'Thou art my hiding-place and my shield'

Anne-Marie had nowhere to go and no money. She walked in her blue dress through the streets of Jerusalem, blinking back her tears of shock, and fighting the work of the sun. She had to take her shoes off and walk barefoot. She felt swollen and heavy by this choice she hadn't asked for.

She'd never felt so alone and so much a stranger. She didn't know how to ask for help, or how she would even say it. The sunlight in their exiled eyes made Israelis squint and snap at tourists. Even if she'd found one who spoke her English or her French, her permanent accent would mark her everywhere as foreign, unreliable, dark.

She stopped to count how much money she had in her purse. Not much. Not enough for the boat that went to nearby Cyprus, not enough for more than three week's rent just about anywhere. For an hour or so she even thought about getting a job like everyone else in the world seemed to have to. She bought a bagel from a bakery chain, which calmed her down despite the unpleasant, sugary taste that bread had in Israel and Palestine, as though they had to pump any little thing they could with sweetness. She caught the hour-long bus to Tel Aviv and called Mohammad from a pay-phone at the coach station.

'Boker tov.'

'Mohammad! Is that how you answer your phone these days?'

'Marie! How are you?' His voice was so simple and kind that she wanted to slam the receiver down and cry. She bit her lower lip: her mouth shaped itself like a turtle's.

'I'm in Tel Aviv. Listen.' She tried to explain to Mohammad about the fight with David, and to convey to him that she was poor and homeless. She reached into her Prada clutch purse to pull out a few more shekels for the phone. She told Mohammad that she was never, ever going back to that man. He didn't say anything back to her for almost a minute.

'Mohammad darling, these silences are expensive.'

'Sorry,' she heard him coming back down to earth for her. 'Catch the 4B bus to Ben Yehuda street. I'll come and meet you. Don't worry, Marie.'

She'd forgotten how soft his voice could be. She wondered if anyone ever heard a word from him in this city, over the cars, the sea and the cat-calls.

\*

Mohammad made up a bed for her in the room next to the kitchen. The apartment had five vague rooms – vague because the rooms had archways instead of doors – perhaps in an economical attempt at making it seem open-plan. It struck Anne-Marie as strange that a man like Mohammad would live in a house where there were not clear compartments. Perhaps when he was on his own he didn't need so many barriers. The bedroom was spacious and up-lit, Mohammad's study calming and clean. The kitchen was a bit steely and bloodless, but it looked like Mohammad knew how to use it, and the main room with the television in was an unpainful shade of off-white and was tidy.

That night, he showed her around the Tel Aviv that he was still learning, like an older orphaned sister – leading the way but still lost. Marie met her first Israelis, properly, at a bar off Allenby Street. Two men her age who came up to her when Mohammad was buying their drinks, to ask her if she was visiting, and if so, where had she been? They were so smilingly interested in her that she offered them the spare chairs at their table. Their jeans were slung lower than David's had been when she had met him aged eighteen.

The taller man had his knotted hair held back with the kind of hair-band Marie wore when she was washing her face. They laughed at her jokes about the weather, and their two different, complimentary smiles were like leaning towers, or like the Jean-Paul Gaultier perfume bottles, which she would have bought in an instant, if only she didn't hate the smell. The one with the hair-band was a DJ. But the other one laughed at her jokes with a sunnier smile. Marie leant towards one and then the other, letting her leg rest against other legs under the table, weighing up various attractions and enjoying the indecisions most of all.

When Mohammad came back, one of the young men greeted him with the kind of punch on the arm that had always struck Marie as embarrassing in American films, but now seemed real and kind. Because they weren't Americans.

The two guys stayed in the spare chairs for twenty minutes, until they said they had to catch a late-night film. When they gave Marie their numbers, she had to turn to Mohammad to check what his telephone number – their telephone number – was, so she could write it on a night-club flyer for the boys. Because this is what you did here: you go to Paris, you see the Eiffel Tower; you go to Israel, you see how many beautiful strong men you can tempt back with your Old World charms. It was the best kind of sight-seeing that she had seen so far.

Walking back Mohammad pointed out an important building, a beautiful building, and Anne-Marie pointed out particularly beautiful girls and men.

'The guys at the bar seemed nice,' Mohammad said, seeming most nervous so far to be alone now with Marie.

'They were.'

'You could've, um. You could've gone out with them if you wanted.'

'No, I wanted to come back with you.'

'OK. Sorry. I just mean . . .'

'Stop worrying, Mohammad.' She smiled at him and they walked home lightly.

\*

Marie's new life with Mohammad was sweet and gentle, but hard to capture in a moment or night. There were very few clear images for her of anything involving Mohammad: it was as though he had to erase them quickly, even from people's memories, as he went along.

Perhaps the two of them cooking: Mohammad would wipe down all the surfaces and ask Marie to bring out what he'd asked her to buy at the market. She liked the way he turned water on to full blast just to wash the vegetables in the giant silver basin. Marie washed her hands diligently, like a child trying to help or enjoying the play-act of helping. And a man got Anne-Marie to chop onions: people would've paid to see it. Mohammad gave her a spoon to bite; he'd heard it worked but never tried it himself. Marie was so pleased with herself for not crying from the onions that she cooked the next night too. The third night, she tried to make broccoli soufflé. She cried over the little burnt cave that she made for so long that it made up for her tearless nights of vegetable chopping.

Mohammad cooked from then on; Anne-Marie did their shopping. And things began to taste of things. Marie had lived on sweets for as long as she could remember, bright and unreal jelly-beans and couture-perfect stripey boiled candy, and in Palestine the food tasted of nowhere – they never ate musakhkan or maqhiba, or whatever Palestinians ate (they weren't even sure); they'd lived off noodles, rice, pasta – and hummus spread inappropriately on everything – as if they were still students. But now Mohammad would always comment that she looked thin, like it wasn't a good thing, which confused her: not that she had the tortuous relationship most girls and women have with food, so much as a bored, abstract distance from the idea of it. But he'd seen her in her days of nightly hunger-pains – he seemed to want to ground her, stop her being restless and jumpy. He'd stop typing at his computer every few hours to chop up some raw carrots and celery, or make a Mediterranean salad, then call her to the kitchen, asking her to eat, or just handing the plate to her and settling back down to work.

Mohammad did his work from his desk at this time,

because the seminars he planned to attend at Tel Aviv University hadn't started yet, and the NGO he was to work with were still sorting out the project he'd be helping with. The only task that his old job had left him was to structure and type up his report on the integration of women's advocacy into UN-sponsored peace initiatives. Marie liked the Amnesty International logo that appeared on letters to Mohammad about his new job even more than she'd liked her old college's stationery.

Marie knew she had to be on her best behaviour in the house, so as not to make Mohammad shy and shaky. So she'd spend the clear days of her first weeks in Israel with a series of the modern paperback novels Mohammad had brought with him from Europe, or walking around the art galleries, and smiling at boys and men on the beach: she'd begun the difficult age of finding both young men and their fathers attractive.

In the evenings she'd read on the largest chair in the room where the television was. She'd walk past Mohammad's study when she went to get a glass of water, or yet another plate of biscuits. She wondered what he was thinking as his eyelids shone in the light of his computer.

One evening she knocked on the wall next to the oval archway where his study door would have been, if he had had one. She wondered whether, if he'd had a door, he would have kept it open when he was working. Mohammad looked up and smiled. He was wearing a black T-shirt that had lasted him since Oxford.

'Hello Marie. Do you want some dinner?'

'No, no it isn't that.' She perched on the edge of his desk and held on to the sides of her skirt. Mohammad saved the changes to the document he was writing, and turned his office-chair towards her, slightly.

'How's your work going?' Marie ventured.

'Oh, you know . . .'

'Listen. Mohammad. I have to talk to you about something.' She tugged her skirt all the way over her knees and swung her legs under the desk until they hit a hiding stack of his Geneva notes.

'What's the matter?'

'Mohammad . . .'

'Yes.'

'I'm twenty-two.'

'I see.' He didn't see. He seemed worried that he was expected to know what to do now. Marie tapped her lips with her hand, and fidgeted with her legs again.

'I think it might be time for me to get a job.'

Mohammad called a colleague in Brussels who'd edited the monthly campaign magazine sent out to Britain's Amnesty International members. He didn't have any room for an unknown writer on his new 'internationalist/ecologist/liberal' publication, but knew someone at an English newspaper who was running a series on how modern war affects women. Marie would be free to write about either Israel or Palestine as she saw fit. She had no idea how war affected women, but the publisher reassured her that no one else did either.

Mohammad gave over his study to her, for her to write the initial article, and carried most of his stacks of law review print-outs to the dining table, making sure to clear it half an hour before the time that he thought Marie might be getting hungry.

Marie sat in his office chair. She spun around in it a lot. It was the most fun you could have in a room full of white-paper reports on war crimes. But after five days, it was only very mildly amusing. A day before the deadline, she'd taken to swinging in the chair so that the sides of her ankles slammed into the desk legs. Mohammad had stopped coming in to the room in answer to her cries of pain, after the third time, when she'd snapped at him to go away.

But then he heard a cry come out from the study. He came running in this time, his highlighter pen left unlidded on the dining room table.

'What's the matter?'

'Mohammad, I can't do it. I can't.' He looked at her quietly, if looks are quiet. 'I said I can't do it!' She was crying, but her expensive mascara stayed in place.

'Hey, hey, you're just nervous.'

'I'm going to be sick.'

'Shh. Shh.' He put his hand on hers too softly: an annoyance. 'I'm sure it'll be fine.' He felt her hand shaking.

'Mohammad, I'm pretending. And now it's too late. I'm pretending to be clever, and if I . . . write this, everyone will know, everyone . . . will know . . .' she spoke in between the rhythmical gasps for air that her sobbing had drummed deep into her lungs.

'Ssh. Marie. Ssh. That's what you always said at Oxford, too.'

'Exactly.'

'But that was just there.'

'It's what I always said in Paris too. It's just that no one heard me there.'

'But you're older now. Come on, Marie. Come on, you can do this.'

And so Mohammad sat with her until four-thirty in the morning, as together they extracted the two thousand words from her, like a tooth, or a mountain rescue airlift.

# AIN

'Leave me not to mine oppressors'

The night Marie heard the news that her article would defi-nitely be printed, Mohammad brought two bottles of wine home for the two of them to celebrate. Marie wondered what he'd looked like buying them. She didn't want to embarrass him by either watching him as he turned the corkscrew uncertainly, or by offering to take over. He poured two glasses for Marie and himself, holding them over the sink.

She poured the next four, while he mopped up the drops that she left on the kitchen counter that was cleaner than a treaty. They sat on the dining room chairs, then the dining room table, as Marie became too animated with some story that her grandmother had once told her to keep her feet on the floor.

They both set their final drinks down, and Marie's glass knocked Mohammad's with a nervous clink. 'I'm sorry,' she said. Her eyes were soft with wine. 'No, it's my fault.' She kissed him to show him that it wasn't. He kissed her back, to show that it was, he was sorry, she kissed him back, he kissed her back again, each little kiss half an instance or less, neither of them opening their mouths up. Her hand was barely on his waist, his hand was barely on the back of her head, their knees were barely touching at the edge of the laden table – but still they were, only just. The table held up like a ship's galley. The corridor melted like spring.

Marie wondered if everybody else in the world had had a moment as tender as when they had made love for the first time, and Mohammad lay his head on her shoulder, while she kissed and kissed his hair with both their eyes closed. She wanted everybody else in the world to send her a letter on crisp white paper that told of a moment in their life that was as soft, and as quiet.

*

The next morning – which Marie had silently wondered about all through the night – was soft and quiet and nice. Mohammad got dressed while she was still asleep, and covered her with the sheets, sparing any embarrassment of his feelings or her beauty. He went down to a bakery to buy her croissants, but could only find bagels and breadsticks at the three shops that he tried. By the time he came back she had showered and looked a simpler, less pained kind of pretty, as she combed her hair on the bed.

She suggested that he show her Tel Aviv's art galleries. Anne-Marie had taken to pretending she was interested in art, and it was a way to do something new together without touching directly on the new thing they had done the night before. They walked in the heat to the Helena Rubinstein pavilion. In the artificially cooled room of the gallery, wherein was playing a video installation, they sat side by side and faced the screen of the artwork.

Mohammad put his hand on hers, or, rather, picked up her hand and placed it in his own, like a puppet's, but gently as grass growing. Marie leant her head on his shoulder. This was the first time that she had done this. But his shoulder and his smell were both so familiar that she felt as though she was returning.

They walked out of the art gallery holding hands, like children, but Mohammad still all tall-looking. Their bodies flinched as one at the wave of heat that had been waiting outside to hit them. That evening they unmade Anne-Marie's bed in the spare room, and put Mohammad's box of law books back to where they used to live before her.

Mohammad and Marie making love was like careful needlepoint, slow as cycling, every night when he was not so worn from his study that he had to hold his eyelids open to watch the evening news. Anne-Marie was supposed to be writing her second successful article. But she was too full of plans for day-trips to Jaffa, and too full of the chocolates and pastries and olives that she kept running out and buying as presents for him and then eating for herself. At night, her stomach singing happily with food, Mohammad would hold her and undress her in the darkness, with the kind of barely-there kisses that were like bubbles popping on her skin. Like a man, she'd watch his pretty face when he was asleep, and feel that he must somehow be being sustained by her gaze alone. His chest went up and down for nothing solid. Perhaps he had no inner monologue, she thought. It was like watching snow fall into the sea.

\*

Marie disturbed Mohammad in his study for the first time since they had started sleeping together to say: 'The news says someone's bombed London.' She'd been watching television when she was supposed to be working. She did not listen to the facts. It took Mohammad, on his laptop, to learn from news websites the key phrases: 'home-grown suicide bombers', 'explosives in plastic water-bottles', 'Edgware Road'.

Then they sat in front of the television all day: they didn't know what things looked like before the BBC World red banner ran across the screen of the whole world. They didn't cry. Mohammad looked tired, like the incoming information had made him run along the beach and all the way up to Jaffa. Marie just bit her lip. All her memories of London were Mohammad and David and the Trafalgar Square lion. Mohammad and David. Mohammad who was here with her; David who was in enemy territory.

No one cried in Tel Aviv streets, either, the way they did in other cities that night, with candles and their Faithless CDs. Murder in Europe was old news here, modern terror everyday and boring. Mohammad skipped the English papers at breakfast for the next two weeks, they were kept informed instead through the indirect voice of *Le Monde* and *Le Nouvel Observateur*. Reading about London in another language was like hearing something private and soft spoken through Marie's strange accent.

\*

And so it was that two and a half weeks later, after spending the morning attending to Marie, pale in bed and crying from the dull, gnawing ache of her period, Mohammad sat down in his study to try to write a letter to David. He was inspired by the days after they bombed London, when Mohammad checked the photographs of victims to make sure David's family were safe. It seemed like the sort of time for some kind of contact.

He took out a pen he'd been given in Geneva. He took out some paper that he had had for forever. He tried to write, in his small hand:

*I love Marie*

*I love you like a brother*

But his writing crumpled, as if it was eating itself. He squinted at the page. Maybe his eyes weren't good. Or maybe his hand was sore from typing. Even he wasn't sure what it said, in the lines that followed his neat address in the top corner.

He couldn't write a word; the situation remained unexplained. He sat at the desk until the sun went down on the balmy Friday night that he'd only brushed against for a moment or two, by the window. He saw that it hadn't touched Marie at all, as she slept, tear-marked and crumpled, in her Pringle jumper and her hand-knitted socks.

He blinked and breathed and rubbed his eyes, trying to focus. He tried to think of the way in which he might be able to explain things to David. Instead he found he could not even explain it to himself.

What he really wanted to ask David for was: orders. He needed commands and advice. He couldn't mention the politics of their on-going situation. Could not tell him that, like a new country, he couldn't think what to do with his freedom now, knowing that all the mistakes he would make with Marie would only ever be his. As he gave up, he remembered: David had never given him his address in Palestine anyway.

He saw he'd filled the waste-paper basket up with his failing thoughts and attempts at explaining, and as he turned the desk lamp of his study off, his head was empty and his whole body ached. He yawned and he saw for a moment what it must be like to be Marie.

*Dear Delilah,*

*I think I should have begun all my letters with the lion and the sweetness that I found. Everyone wants to be a Biblical lion – hard outside and filled with honey – except for me.*

*I never told you about it. You didn't trick all of my secrets out of me, and I'm sorry. It happened one day, as I was walking to meet my wife. I killed the lion months before, but I never forget a victory – just like all those men you hate, only with G-d in me. I preferred to detour to a site of one of my former triumphs than meet the woman who waited for me – just like all those men you hate, only with G-d in me. I pushed the carcass over to see its remains. Just like all those men you hate, who do not flinch from the sight of anything.*

*I didn't flinch from what I found, I did not jump back from the bees, as I scooped the honey into my palms, and licked them with my tongue. I did not flinch – I was commanded to place it in my mouth. This is what He wanted to teach me: that all sweetness is strange. And that His work is done in all things that make you hungry and full.*

*You know, don't know, what people think of us. But my love with G-d was more physical than ours. It felt like He was feeling the world through my body, like a glove, with one less layer of skin than He wears even in children and creatures. He let me taste the things that live forever – the way that taste and smell bring back* mortal men's dreams, so too the taste of His creation stayed on my tongue even as I touched the marble of the towers.

*Do not let my soul die with the Philistines. Let my soul live, as the song says,* and it shall praise thee; and let thy judgements help me. I have gone astray like a lost sheep; seek thy servant; for I do not forget thy commandments. *I can't forget it. It is stuck in my teeth.*

*This is the other reconciliation I'm seeking, Delilah. Which I am seeking through a letter to you. I love Him, I know that now, but I had to learn how to love Him for myself. In the Qur'an, Adam and Eve are only placed on earth, forgiven, once they've shown they can make independent thoughts: this is what He loves, that we'd choose to love Him. I had to learn it through the world, not the path he paved. I think you understand this, Delilah, the having to go it alone. Everyone is a son, in their fashion. You always said that that was how you felt.*

*I love Him; I love you. And I hope I can give the things I love all I have; I hope they leave me nothing for myself. All that is lost is found again. I did not know where to look to find the missing pieces of my heart: it's very handy that He sees everything, for people as forgetful as you and me. I was waiting, like Sappho's fragments, to be alchemised back into love.*

The Dead Sea Scroll Song

You cannot get there by sea:
*the water is trapped.*
You cannot get there by maps
*for the name is a trap in itself.*
You cannot get there by books:
*there are no pages*
to start with.

You cannot get there through the city,
*it lives like Arafat*
its house is a bunker
*in a boxed Hebrew letter*
guarded by Alephs
*that prickle like pear-cactus*
and cannot be cut.

And so you wander
*the streets in the sun*
the space where your understanding should be
*yawning and yawning*
like the entrance of an Omega,
*a gap in the mark that your shape is making*
here upon the white of Jerusalem,
*and keeps on yawning*
like a soldier at a checkpoint,
*until you are empty*
as a cave
*and are stumbling upon things*
like an illiterate.

*You were the only one who sought me out, Delilah. You exca-
vated me from the places where I had buried myself. Or else you
stumbled upon me, like the Bedouin boy in the cave of scrolls, but
kept what you learnt to yourself. Taught yourself how to read it,
and recited it nightly.*

*It was a real, human miracle for me: nobody else had ever
wanted to know who I really was. You wanted to know everything.
'What is your secret? What is your strength? What would you be
without it? Show me. Show me.' Everyone else shirked from that
mortal cement in me, that which held the pillars of His house up.*

It felt like they'd covered half my body with a tent. But you loved me and wanted me for me.

I brought you to the banqueting house, and my banner over you was love, as the Song of Songs goes. I brought you there, but to worship Him.

So now love me for the part that He is too. Like you would ask of a man: love me for all of me. Loving each other every day is nothing if not for being His mirror. The way that you would ask me to sit and help you put on your mascara. Without us loving for each other and for Him, our bodies will melt with heaviness, like a cargo of unsung songs, run aground on the wrong shore. Love me for Him, set Him as a seal upon thine heart, as a seal upon thine arm. With your left hand under my head, and my right hand embracing me, as it says in the song, in the Song of Songs, in the song which is also a prayer. His statutes have been my song in the house of my pilgrimage, and His holy arms are wide enough to hold every way we have of worshipping.

## PE

'Rivers of waters run down mine eyes,
because they do not keep thy law'

The weather changed. Marie was surprised that, in this heat and in this city, she could still sense the seasons performing their acts. But new winds came from the Mediterranean, bringing with them the songs that Israel had almost forgotten. It pecked like kisses at the chipped buildings, rattled gently the iron railings of the Mandate-era balconies, rocked the edges of the sea like a polite tapping on the shoulder, to say: you dropped this, sir, excuse me, you forgot something. From the balcony, Anne-Marie watched whole streets of men run as the breeze blew off their various hats, or girlishly fiddling, the way that she did, with hair pins behind their masculine heads, to save their yarmulkes. She and Mohammad would walk along different stretches of the sand, and watch the changes in the line where the sea would stroke the sky.

'Kiss me here.' He did as he was told. She got him to lie down with her.

'Kiss me here.'

'Marie.'

'Kiss me.'

'Marie, people might see us.'

'They won't.'

'They might.'

Many of Marie's happinesses were sacrificed on the altar of how sharp the eyes of passing Israelis might have been. She wanted to throw rocks through the windows of the opticians, rattle like the wind at the houses on the shore. She'd kiss him on the beach and he'd look around to see if anyone was offended.

'What's the matter?'

'Nothing.'

'Mohammad, if you don't want me to kiss you, just say so.'

'Of course I do. I'm sorry, Marie.'

An apology for kissing was the worst thing, so she'd slip into a silence of biting her fingernails. He'd look hurt that she'd retreated, so she'd say with a cruel casualness: 'Forget it. Let's go home.'

She hadn't always wanted to shake Mohammad in this way. He was so shy, and boundaries sprung up so often and even without a word, that she didn't want to alarm him even with the strength of his own feelings. Sometimes she'd avoid certain things in sex that would give him too much pleasure, and so make it unbearable. It was a strange new way of loving for her, to love someone by not scaring them with feeling love. She loved him and wanted to show him how to love her back. She thought this kind of teaching was a gift for him.

She'd tried her best to leave him alone when they were in the house together. As she now had her own, occasional, work, which she'd write sitting on their tidy bed, the two would be in their separate rooms during the day, for writing and for research, and then would come out into the dining room for meals. They agreed to finish work at seven o'clock every evening, to talk and have a glass of wine. Their pretence at being adults grew into the real thing without too many difficulties, like a little climber plant growing up upon a trellis. They kept buying every kind of newspaper that they could, mixing the spirits of languages, maturing and churning their opinions.

Lying on the bed to write her articles, unable as ever to concentrate, Anne-Marie at first thought that it was the glass of wine she was looking forward to so much that she couldn't write. She spent an hour worrying about how her skin would sag if she became an alcoholic, and from then on Mohammad bought too-sweet Jaffa orange juice from the Arab man near the Carmel market for their evenings, instead of wine. Still Marie was restless, and listened enviously to the clicking of Mohammad's computer keys, which scurried through the quiet house, like nibbling mice or like children that they'd forgotten to have.

She missed Mohammad, she realised, when he went out to buy the olive oil they'd forgotten to replace earlier. She missed him even when he was in the house. She missed him so much that all she did all day was doodle and write the title of her latest article next to her name, or his name, over and over. She missed him because it never felt as if he was there.

And so she began to press him, not to hurt him exactly, but to know him, to get the panorama, to find a border or a sea. They'd been sleeping together for months, and still she wondered what his face would look like agitated. She knew she loved him but didn't know him well enough to be sure of how he'd react to hearing it said: casually, sober, when they were dressed. She knew that she knew him, that he was familiar as language, but still she spent whole sleepless nights wondering what he might be dreaming.

But what could she do to win him to her? She'd only ever questioned her powers when it came to the English girls in the English bookshop – even the Palestinian girls were bought off with her charm and cheating secrets eventually – and the Israeli boys were bought off with little more than her sweets and her sweet accent. Mohammad had known her so well and for so long before he'd even kissed her. She didn't know how to begin again.

She couldn't take up cooking, so instead she took up buying things. The whole house stank of food. Like tubes of brilliant paints that mixed together turn to brown, a smudgy aura of every part of the digestive process seeped through the fridge and the fruit bowls that Anne-Marie had placed in every room except the bathroom. The furniture was replaced, excitingly, piece by piece, with her own money, for the first time in her life. The walls were hung with Israeli art: clever and clean and barely there at all. And all these objects and altered settings were summoned to take her side in a dance that Mohammad didn't even know he'd asked her hand for.

When he was fasting Marie would chase him, sweetly, with the brioche bought from the best patisserie. She ran through the house, tickling him, and pressing him down laughingly, trying to catch him and then trying to open his mouth, and then telling him to open his mouth, and then not understanding why he wouldn't open his mouth, and then demanding that he open his mouth, and then forcing him to open his mouth, because by then it wasn't funny any more and then she would start to shout:

*Well why are you fasting, how old are you, of course I think it's stupid, how can you still believe in it, you went to Oxford, you're a rational human being, you love me remember, you love me don't you, don't you get hungry, don't you laugh at yourself, why won't you answer, why don't you want me.*

And every time she harmed him with herself like this, still she thought that she could heal him with herself, if only there was enough of it. And so through their house she became as omnipresent as the black flies that had come after the fruit bowls. She'd try to baptise him in an immersion of kisses: as he worked, as he slept, as he brushed his teeth while wearing his faded blue T-shirt that was already drenched in kisses. He couldn't sit at his desk for an hour without her beautiful arms reaching round his tensing shoulders and back. Her perfume was everywhere and her lips were mechanical. She was eternally stroking his sleeping head, or sometimes pretending to be peaceful, in the hope that he would wake, and when he did not wake, kicking him playfully, and when he turned over, playfully, funnily, firmly, then forcibly turning him back and saying: 'Talk to me.'

Or else she was running up the stairs, her arms full of presents and shouting of plans from them to go to the beach. He didn't know how to reply, but he would often clear his throat, or scratch a part of his head that had so far been spared her pecking kisses.

'Darling, *please*,' she'd say.

'Marie, please,' he'd say with sad quietness, if he was typing, or cooking, waving her away, softly, with a movement of a hand that he thought was gentleness. He was impotent when it came to anger. He didn't seem to try very hard to understand her, but instead let her get away with every petulant act that she wanted him to take issue with.

Some afternoons she'd come into the study in expensive underwear, as he tapped diligently away on his lap-top. He'd try to carry on working as before, casting her a meek smile, lit by computer-glow, or take her hand softly and whisper in earnest as she shivered in her bra:

'Um, Marie, you're sitting on my report for Amnesty.'

'If you loved me you'd kiss me.'

'SHUT UP SHUT UP, YOU STUPID WOMAN, LET ME HAVE TWO WHOLE FUCKING SECONDS OF PEACE AND QUIET' is what Mohammad never suddenly shouted as Marie's main task of any day became to push and push, make him kiss her, wind him up, as he tried to do his job, his chores and eat three meals when appropriate.

'I don't want you anyway. I was just bored.'

These were the cruellest words that anyone had ever said to him, and he went and made himself a cup of tea. Eventually Marie would sit in burning defeat and cry her bitter tears on to their newly bought furniture. The house's chairs were cold and corrective, the cushions all like ossuaries. It was the time of the last round of removals of the settlers from the West Bank, and Anne-Marie watched the unbearably slow retreat filter through the early-hour news broadcasts. She screwed up her toes and tensed her insides at the footage of the soldiers dragging off the little children. She could not even cry by then – it was so much the opposite of pleasure that it was not even pain. She forcibly held her eyes open like Mohammad did after he'd done too much work.

Night after night, she made herself sit bitterly upright. She stared sleeplessly through the news updates, and bit her lip through all of the agony of the peace.

# TZADDI
'My zeal hath consumed me'

It seemed to take a supernatural effort to heat the world up again that spring. The world was growing stale: the times they lived in were now the background, the ongoing fact. Girls who'd lost their virginity the day before the planes were crashed – guilty-feeling, secret sixteen-year-olds – would have grown somehow into women by now, and the clothes this year's sixteen-year-olds were wearing were different from Marie's. It was strange to no longer be on the precipice of the times, and all it's indicators of politics and hemlines. Marie thought of David, his low trousers that showed his hip bones and his underwear – teenage clothes – and wondered whether he still wore them now, as a grown man who'd made a choice to be one thing and not another. It seemed appropriate now that his family had been wearing black when they said goodbye to him at university: burying a boy who could be anything, who still hadn't chosen yet. She thought about these things as she familiarised herself with the new angles of the city, this year's clothes, and over-heard Hebrew slang that she wouldn't ever get to use: she was an observer only in this city, documenting it silently for no one.

But then, then, summer came back, almost unexpect-edly, a sad miracle of life just going on: bare legs everywhere, more music than ever, and parties and parties all across the Tel Aviv beaches. Men flirted with Marie, making use of what mutual languages they could, when she went for her walks, alone, by the sea. The music coming from the beach-front shops – divided by which had been bombed, and which were still awaiting it – Marie understood the rhythm of, moved in time to as she walked. Perhaps, after all, they were still young. She tried to hold on to this thought as she made her way back to Mohammad.

*

Anne-Marie and Mohammad lay in bed, reading the papers. The lamp hung down like a suction mask. The war had broken out between Israel and Lebanon five days earlier, and, that evening, the two were still digesting the incoming news. War was, to them, like being a thirteen-year-old girl: everything important happened three streets away, but you weren't invited, and had to wait until the morning to hear about it. There was no real suggestion that Tel Aviv would be bombed – except in the *Jerusalem Post*, which Mohammad read first and tried to hide from Marie – but still neither of them could sleep or do anything useful with their hands or head.

'Would you like me to turn the light out?'

'If you like, here's a good place to stop what I'm reading.'

'OK. Goodnight, then.'

They hadn't made love for over six weeks. As Marie lay in the darkness, holding herself like the sleeping arm of another person, she tried to think beyond her bad behaviour – which was easy for her, she didn't want to dwell on her image in the unflattering light of moral sense or cheap magazines – and look to why else Mohammad might have retreated from her so completely, as if a lovely war was over.

Perhaps he didn't find her attractive? She had no access to the comparative element that determined female beauty: she'd never seen him so much as look at any other woman or girl. It had been a favourite game, in Oxford, to watch him react as she pointed to this girl or that, who was 'totally in love with you'. Maybe, she wondered, he thought that she was still in love with David, that he was just the sky that the earlier love circled in, the minor variation of the song. And it was true that still the deepest parts of her small heart, even more than it said Chan-el Chan-el Chan-el, or just said her own voice mindlessly, it sang David David David David, and that the faster anything made her heart beat – any running or bomb-scares or sex – the closer it brought David back to her, the more it dug him into her chest. Perhaps Mohammad didn't want to hold her in a way that brought somebody else back. It also occurred to her briefly: perhaps she reminded him of someone more alpha, whom he'd loved first, and couldn't forget.

The next day, she moved her things back into the spare room while Mohammad sat at the desk. She guessed he'd heard her carrying things and decided not to come out and help. It seemed less painful, somehow, to go back to how they'd been for years, as quiet friends, than to lie side by side in the silence for another night of the wrong sort of heat, and the hymn of air conditioning. She'd already memorised all the marks on that bedroom ceiling.

A small bed is better for a little soul. She tucked herself in like a baby: the bed-sheets were crisp like unlicked envelopes, and she tried to dream she was posting herself somewhere pure. The first few nights in the new room, she'd keep reminding herself that she didn't need to cry quite so quietly now, if she didn't want to. She listened to the Neon Bible and watched the ceiling with a certain interest. Some nights when she felt worn but sleepless, she'd go out on to the balcony and watch the city she didn't know, thinking of the people who she'd never really understood, and it felt almost like even Tel Aviv had stopped loving her now. She would lean far out against the railing, with a cigarette that made her feel sick, or breathing in the night air, or just leaning, towards anything that would respond.

She thought about moving out of the apartment completely. The idea of her living alone seemed impossible: but so too had it once seemed to live without her grandmother, live without David, write a whole page of her own words without biting her palm until it bled. It was a case of having no imagination, not of anything else. She decided to talk to Mohammad about it that evening, and so cooked their light lunch while he was out shopping. It was the least she could do.

Mohammad came through the door as she finished cutting the sad-looking salad and pouring out two glasses of wine. The heat of the city followed him, and Marie came out of the kitchen in response to it. Just as she saw the look on his face, she followed it, and joined it, like a constellation, to the figure of the professor. He hovered in their door-frame like the medieval marking of the plague.

'Mohammad? What's happened?'

'Nothing, Marie, don't worry.'

'Let me talk to her,' the professor's voice came out. It was just the same. It was as hard to forget as language. Every-thing came back to you, in the right environment.

Mohammad looked pale and his eyes flickered, as he turned between the figure in the entrance and Anne-Marie, with her palms together and to her lips, in front of them both, suddenly as tiny as though kneeling.

'Marie, why don't you go and see if the food is ready?' Mohammad's voice tried.

'It's fucking ready, Mohammad. What's going on? Why is he here?'

Then Mohammad put his palms to his face and made a noise that could have been a cry. The professor caught Marie's eye. She saw he'd crossed the border he'd lived on for so long, and was now indisputably old, just old; wasn't on holiday in that age, but had gone there and would never come back. Mohammad would have been taller than him, then, if his shudders hadn't forced him to stoop and bow his head.

Then Mohammad looked up and took a deep breath as he rubbed his eyes in resignation. 'OK. OK.' He took another breath. 'He's going to tell you something, Marie. He's going to tell you something awful. And when you hear it, I want you to try to be calm, I want you to try to . . .' She had never heard the phrase 'I want you' come from his lips before.

'Just let him tell me.'

'Oh God.' Other possible-cries followed from him.

'Marie.' The professor suddenly stepped out from behind Mohammad, and took her to the hungry table that was still awaiting food. 'I made an error of judgement. I have tried to put it right, and I am sorry.'

'It's David, isn't it? What's happened?'

'Would you just *listen* to me?' The professor snapped. This was a strange time for impatience. It brought back everything about the professor that his worn face and clothes had not already carried into her thoughts.

'That library that you two lived in . . .'

'Yes . . .'

'I had several plans for it, originally. It was always going to be a library, but there were other things we could do with it too. It was so big . . .'

'OK . . .'

'So. One of the other things we were going to do with it was hide weapons there.'

'What? What do you . . .Who is "we"?'

'Never mind, Marie. Anyway, we didn't. We decided it was too risky, to have weapons so close to Israel, even though in some ways it was perfect, as Hezbollah could then . . .'

'Wait, Hezbollah weapons? Not Hamas?'

'It's too complicated to explain.' Sweet Maria, so blonde and so platinumly useless, there was no way of getting your hands underneath her ignorance, this would all have to unfold before her like a first-rate play put on by college students. The professor seemed to try to explain, anyway, if only to stop Anne-Marie's awful staring – Palestine is a non-state, he said, so it's often easier for criminal activity; besides, when Syria left Lebanon some feared that the new Lebanese democracy might cause a few problems to their activities, and the library was just sitting there . . . this drifted past Marie and, for the most part, Mohammad, as landscape does to those in a car.

'The point is, Marie, now the war's broken out, and Hezbollah aren't a proper army or anything, they're going to want to get at any weapons they can. I think they're going to try to take Jerusalem. I flew here because a contact demanded that I tell them where they were.'

'But you said they weren't even in the library.'

'Yes, but that doesn't matter. They'll go round to find them. They'll break in, and if anyone tries to stop them,' the professor didn't flinch, 'they will shoot them.'

'But . . .' She did not know where to begin. 'But why? Why did you let him live there if this could have happened? Why did you let me? Why did you . . .'

'Marie, Marie, I didn't know there was going to be a war with Lebanon.'

'And I suppose a nice Jewish boy was a fairly good decoy for a hiding place, if there was one.'

'I'm hardly the only person who's ever used David Cohen.'

'Why . . .' She looked as if she was going to hit him. But she could hardly even stand. 'Why do you hate David?'

'He doesn't.' Mohammad stood over them, at an equal distance. 'Or, at least, he didn't. David told me in Sarajevo . . . he thought you'd guessed. He said he went to Palestine for him.' Marie received this news like a President receiving a piece of paper from an aide: the assistant slid it in front her, she didn't look to the side to acknowledge it. The professor's face was unchanged. Did the professor's face ever change? She didn't think about anything.

'So what now? What can we do about it?'

'Nothing. It's too, absolutely too, dangerous to go into Palestine now to reach him, even if we try to contact him and he flees, there's no knowing someone isn't watching him, and will force him to tell them where the weapons are.'

'But there aren't any weapons! Why did you let him live there? You invited him into that house, and it was . . . why did you let him live there? Without telling him that this might happen? There must be something we can do, some way I can get to him, and explain to him, or take him through the border, or . . .'

'No,' the professor said firmly, 'I came here because I thought there was something I could do. But it's turning into a real war – who knows how a real war will affect things between Israel and Palestine, let alone anything else.'

'But if we do something now, before anything else develops . . .'

'There's nothing we can do,' Mohammad said. 'If there was, we'd be doing it.'

'And you.' She turned to the second pillar. 'You were going to stop him from telling me this?'

'I just . . .' he put his arms out to Marie. His face had crumpled like paper. 'I knew that you'd get like this, I wanted to sort it without you. And then, when I realised we couldn't sort it, I knew telling you would make you do something dangerous. I couldn't let you run off into a war, a real proper war, and not . . .'

'You couldn't let me go back to David.'

As she tried to leave the house, she grabbed a pair of her shoes by the door: her gold Greek lace-up sandals that she'd bought from the dirty market. She looked around for something more practical, then seemed to remember – she was Marie, she had nothing practical. She struggled sobbing for almost a minute, trying to tie the shining laces, as the professor looked on neutrally as a minor God, and as Mohammad put his arms out and pleaded with her.

He tried to get between her and the door, but he was not very practised at this sort of strength. Anne-Marie's shoes slipped slightly from being laced up badly, and she tripped, then grabbed the handle of their door.

'Marie, please, I love you.'

'Oh fuck off, Mohammad.'

The professor made three attempts at a sentence before leaving without finishing any of them. Mohammad sensed a lie in something he had said, about who owned the weapons, about who did this, about what would happen, but he could not question or speak.

# RUMI

In our flight from the Mongols, our caravan passed through Damascus, and as a young man I heard many tales of Jerusalem: its beauty, its horrors, its truth and its lies – and all these relayed to me by men both lying and truthful – it became as a whole universe in my mind: God kept one eye on this little place, and the other eye on everything.

And it felt as though I'd lived there, and that it was really my home. We reprimand those who think they know a place, think they've solved it like a maths equation, without even stepping foot on it. We're all weary of those who colonise with their minds. But Jerusalem, Jerusalem, I knew as a young man, was an idea more than it was a city, and that's how it could be my home. And you can come to this conclusion with maths, after all: if you count how many people live there, have ever lived on those hills of the city, to how many people, century after century, time after time, have dreamt of it, built it into their most important prayers, inhabited it in their exiled dreaming: you realise – Jerusalem really exists somewhere other than on those hills. Jerusalem exists in a country of the mind.

If the journey from Baghdad strained me especially, it was not so much because my legs were eight-hundred-years unfit, so much as I was travelling across the line between Jerusalem the idea and Jerusalem the city. The real journey was difficult, but that is an obvious fact. Travel should be difficult: why else ever arrive? The details – of the night I fell and two young men carried me, of the times I dreamt feverishly and hated to wake, of the blood that came variously out of my feet, my mouth, my sides – these you can imagine for yourself. Harder to pinpoint would be the long journey of my mind then, the unexpected turns, the sudden difficulties encountered, in coming to Jerusalem for the first time, finally returning to somewhere I had never been. 'We are all returning,' I once wrote: and as often happens, I began to understand my own words only after they have inhabited the world for a time, and then are set back down once more before me.

And Jerusalem was as I expected it to be. We reprimand people who say this when they travel. We demand they be surprised, their views changed – this is what we leave our homes and homelands for. But Jerusalem was familiar as breathing. All the prayers, like little faces, flowers in the sun – leaning out and begging, wide-eyed and desperate – feed me, feed me, feed me, like little lost birds in a nest. Jerusalem was my heart written large: like an epic story, the many voices in me found peace only when they were given to many different figures, many creeds and dreams. I stroked the new buildings and the old buildings with an equal love – all their differences balanced out into me.

Every country at war has a different smell. Jerusalem smelt of the effort people made, perfumes and new clothes, to comfort themselves, when the war in their north threatened to break the hard-won island of peace, bought with so many, here and elsewhere. I walked down the streets which felt like mine, and then remembered how everyone feels this about Jerusalem. I walked to the Jewish library: modern books, modern people, buzzing machines watching over them. But this was not the library Samson and Delilah spoke of – this was not the library I was meant to be inside, perhaps already was inside, a closed-book secret biding my time on its shelves. This library felt like a marketplace.

I walked east in the heat, rare different heat of Jerusalem, feverish, to an old Muslim library, but it didn't even contain me – I could smell it, and sense the lack: they did not extend their canopy to the imprecision of holy love. I was neither needed nor wanted there. I could read some looks upon some faces, but that was the extent of my shared knowledge with them. Not so very much for brothers. And it hurt more even than the library in Baghdad, that this one had not been destroyed so much as slowly strangled. An old man pushed me out the door as I stood there looking at nothing.

I walked to the outskirts of the city with these thoughts on my shoulders, feeling suddenly too old, and too old at least to be lost. The angel-devils had distanced themselves from me, had filed themselves into two lines somewhere, as though their sentencing had finally begun. I felt more alone than I ever had in my cave, my centuries where I thought I'd mastered loneliness and made a friend in it. I felt like Samson, unable to understand what my command was, what God wanted of me, and what I could do. I felt like Delilah, trying to reach God beyond the imperfect world of images, but having no other language to understand it in. I walked beyond the city, through the fields of olives and rust, life and the attempts on it, to a new town of its own smell.

'Where is the library?' I asked God.

'Something terrible will happen. What can I do to prevent it?' I asked God.

'I do not have infinite wisdom. What can I do to help? What do I need to learn?'

God didn't answer and I leant against a wall, painted by children, listening to the guns that had suddenly arisen within. I had come too late to change anything at all. I was old and nobody understood my language; I am old and still can't find a way alone, to even begin to try to help. I listened to the guns that sang from inside of the library, and understood the message and the song. Because God does not always answer you: it doesn't mean anything at all.

# SCHIN
'Great peace have they which love'

Marie paced towards the beach, to which all roads led in her neighbourhood. She needed to get herself to the sea, but her long white dress and slipping shoes meant that she might not even reach the edge of the sand.

The sun had been sweating over the shoreline all morning, which quivered like the outward signs of an old dog's nightmare. Human shades of bodies filled the full length of the beach, but not the sea. From the road she saw an empty lifeguard-tower impotently shadowing a section of the sand: this was to be her wise and guiding star.

Aeroplanes that were headed for Ben Gurion airport began their buzzy and brief descents facing the most central sections of the beach front, deeply low and as head-on as a bullfight. Marie had long since learnt not to flinch when watching a plane descend on a city, and she guessed that the Israelis had never bothered to acquire another daily dose of terror. She reached the busy road that hugged the shoreline all across the city: the sea and the purest silence were four lanes of traffic away but her feet and her head hurt.

And as she tripped over her own shoes, through her shaken vision she saw a stray cat run out into the road, shocked by the sudden movement of Marie's unreliable feet. The cat ran straight under the wheels of a car. It flew off to one side, and was hit by a taxi from the opposite direction. Marie ran out into the traffic. No cars hit her, and the cat wasn't dead. She leant down and picked it up; its face was bloody, and one side of it looked punctured: it let out the worst cry she had ever heard, but it was alive.

'Slikha!' she yelled to the taxis thundering down the sick-hot tarmac. She tried to put out her hand to hail one, but the creature required both her arms for support. She had to step back into the greasy flow of cars.

'Slikha! Bavakasha!' she forcibly hailed down a taxi from the centre of the lane. The man inside was redder on his nose than his cheeks, in sports sunglasses, and sneering the Tel Aviv sneer of too much sunlight and no time. He looked her up and down with vulgarity. Everything a person would think at the sight of Marie then, he showed in the space between his unshaven lip and his burnt nose.

'Lo lo lo,' he said, and nodded his head at the same time. Nothing made sense to her: perhaps lo meant *yes* in Hebrew and not *no*, she thought. It was all equally possible to her when she felt so beaten with the sun. All her languages had failed. She could feel the driver openly staring at her bright distorted face. She felt her mouth opening up to him.

'Slikha . . . ani rotsa . . . a vet, no a *vet* . . . le chat est . . . bavakasha, shukran . . . but please. But *please*.'

As he drove away she realised that she wouldn't have had the money to pay him anyway. She looked back down to the creature: it was struggling violently. Her arms had been scratched as she was talking to the taxi driver. She set the animal down on the pavement as gently as she could. It tried to walk, dragging its broken leg, but fell down to one side. Blood came out of its arse like a plastic ketchup-bottle being squeezed and it sprayed everywhere, over Marie, over the pavement. It lay on its side as the cars sped past them, stretching its mouth so desperately, to cry, that the veins of its neck were visible, and the strain pushed blood out from the rupture in its side. It was by watching this blood spurt, then stop, that Marie realised that the cat had died.

She leant down to it again, and took it in her arms. She was all alone, and wondered what she was meant to do now. She couldn't bury it in the sand: children were playing there, things would dig it up. She couldn't leave it on the road. She knew better than to ask another Israeli for help, as her front became quickly covered in flecks of fresh blood that had been hiding, like the mudjahadeen, in caves of the dead cat's fur.

And so with the creature's body in her hands, she walked past the plastic beach-front kiosks, and down a street that led into the market. Her vision was stunted with throbbing tears and nausea, and she scraped her right ankle in miscalculating several times when to step off from the sidewalk. The sun beat down on her like debts, and the passing Israelis stared openly.

She stopped to vomit at the edge of the dirty pavement. The streets already smelt of cats, and sick, and cat shit, and even now another gammy-eyed stray was bringing up a chunk of chicken on the other side of the street. The sun in its power activated all the stenches, as though all was spring-time, and these horrors some cornfield in France.

Leaning over to be sick again, she saw the dead cat's organs were coming out on to the front of her dress. Chunks of inside parts she couldn't name either rested against her or draped meaninglessly, and the congealing blood began to stick her clothes to her stomach. She peeled the material away, but it fell back, and Anne-Marie was sick again.

She'd tried to sit but she couldn't balance herself enough even to crouch, and she realised she had no other option but to keep on walking, stumbling in the same direction she had chosen almost blind. She had no free hand to hold her hair back as she vomited. The creature's blood dripped down her ankles and on to her shoes. Her walk was methodical as a funeral procession, her face blotchy and her nose and mouth running like sores.

She began to walk through the market. Everyone stared, or shouted at her, things she did not understand. Where was she going? She looked up from the creature, lost her balance with the trampolining skyline, and fell to the floor in between two stalls of vegetables. One of the stall vendors screamed at her; she pulled herself up with the metal table leg of his stall. She walked towards the centre of the market, where the knock-off Louis Vuitton bags and fake Manchester United shirts waited for her and her offering. She remembered that that was where the giant bins were, that serviced the whole dirty market.

Marching through a narrow pathway, her Greek sandals slipped again, and she fell for a second time, bruising the side of her chest. A young man turned to offer her a hand, and shot a confused look at the cat's body, which had fallen from her hands. As he saw her face, his look turned to disgust. He was the sort of man she'd always found attractive. She pulled herself up, her dress covered with the brown filth of the market floor. People were coming up to look now, as well as pacing away from her. She could not walk any faster or slower, and she stopped at times to vomit where no one stood. At length she made it to the end of the walkway, and turned the corner to where the bins were: there were fewer people here, and it was shaded by a dark tarpaulin above.

Just as the bins came into view – giant, and three shades bluer than the sky – Marie fell down again, unexpectedly. She'd caught one sandal on the other, and it had ripped the straps off her left shoe. They lay in the dirt, their gold mostly covered. She picked up the cat's body again. She crawled the last stretch to the bins on her knees.

She looked up at the containers that she now faced. She supposed her plan or direction had been to place the cat in one of these. She knelt on her hands and knees like a cat. Now she was here, she couldn't even reach up to the lids. She turned again, as painfully as an ocean-liner, to rest her back against the bin. She placed the body down beside her; all the blood had dried. Oh God: this was roughly how she thought. Her head and feet hurt, and the pulse went through them, going: Oh God Oh God Oh God. She got back on her knees to vomit. Things came out of her mouth the same way that they had come out of the cat. She wanted to get all the sickness out of her. Her stomach jolted when there was nothing else to throw up. She retched for a long time into the darkness, and her throat burned: it was a cotton-wool-and-fingernail feeling. Her mouth tasted of vague remembered bodily essentials: of bacon and of limes.

Her jaw ached and had clamped itself open. She didn't have enough to offer the filthy floor of the market.

For causing the death of a cat. For wearing gold Greek sandals. For running out towards the sea. For failing. For not caring enough about anything that wasn't herself, her vague self. For not caring enough about the Palestinians, or seeing all their human nuances; nor caring enough about the Israelis – judging them by higher standards, which they hadn't asked for. For the last words she had said to Mohammad. For the last words she had ever said to David. For her final testament, and for every other stupid word she had said, and every piece of clothing, and every fraudulent gesture, and every practised walk, and limping run, and for running to the sea, and for not reaching the sea, and for caring about cats, for caring about cats, for caring about cats when the country's in a war. For being so blonde and so platinumly useless, so poor at this ethical algebra: to not carry the ones, to not carry anything, she was sick again and she thought of the hatboxes that she had come to Oxford with, that had once housed everything that she was capable of caring for.

Ordinary words failed her still, as she knelt in her sick and the dirt of the market and everything. Her head pulsed as if birthing names: *David Mohammad David Mohammad.* Oh God Oh God Oh God Oh God Oh God. Then, not the professor's name, but the word Professor, and all the words she had written for him mixed with all the words that she hadn't, at the same sick distance away from meaning, they held each other up. All the girls who came to the library: their faces came to her cloaked in reddest headscarves and hit her over and over like candyfloss-drunk dodgem cars. *Marla. Mar-la Mar-la Mar-la*, the blonde girl who was killed in Iraq. Beautiful Marla, her virgin sister, who cared about Arabs, cared about everyone, was not scared, or bored, of tanks or documents. She was sick and guilty for even thinking of them. She was sick and guilty for *not* thinking about the Palestinians, or all the other victims, sick and guilty, so defiled that she could not even *think* about the Palestinians – she, who had lived among them – sick that even her guilt was so blonde and so holy artificial, that even the victims of her visions now were shining and picturesque. How could she get beyond this: beyond the limitations of her little soul, all her heart and all her teachings, get her fingers under her own thoughts somehow, and light the waiting candles of caring for every person she had ever hurt and dismissed?

She remembered the succession of English girls in the bookshop: she'd seen in them, then, what she could not see in herself, and was repelled, sickened by her own attraction, but they were not her mirror. She was sick for having brought them into her story. They were not a Chorus. They were not the ones who had committed the crimes that spilled out on to her clothes. How had she never realised that the world was not a library but a filthy market? What part had she let herself play? She remembered everything she'd ever said: where had she even learnt those words? She remembered all the events she'd lived through – terror-attacks hung like teeth on a necklace – she'd only ever watched the news like ballet. She remembered her part in it, no part too small for judgement now, as though the angel-devils of untried men were finally being pardoned and sentenced in turn. The parts were all being read out: every time she'd supported Israel, when it was wrong; every time she hadn't defended Israel, when it would have been the right thing to do. She didn't know where the line was but she knew now that she was lost. She remembered the face of the screaming man that she'd found downstairs in the library – and it was her own face, scared only for itself, and utterly unlovable. She remembered that her own father was alive, and that he probably loved her still, even after all that she had done. She remembered the words she'd learnt in some other life: *I prevented the dawning of the morning. Rivers of water run down mine eyes, because they keep not thy law. My flesh trembleth for fear of thee, and I am afraid of thy judgements. Let my soul live, and it shall praise thee; and let thy judgements help me. I have gone astray like a lost sheep; seek thy servant, for I do not forget thy commands, Oh my God. Oh God Oh God Oh God Oh God.*

*Dear Samson,*

*It is not so cold, or not nearly so cold, in this room where I sit now I've learnt to make fire. I wish I could watch myself do it, as if I was somebody else. But I have to do it all alone. First I block the mouths of the drunk wine-bottles: I feed them with the thousands of wishless paper rolls. I've been saving up both. I rip up every scroll, dip it in oil, and, stuffing them into the tops of the bottles, bottle myself up.*

*I will be the chief curator of this encyclopaedic forgetting. I wedge these sinews of the books between myself and the people of books. And this is what I have been doing, Samson: what I do during the day. The piece of paper you're holding now is the only one I have left.*

*I know a person can't stop a whole language: it can take on more forms than even you can, and just as you raise a sword to it, it turns it into a sigh. I'm not trying to re-do the writing on these little papers, so that, in the future, they'll only fight for my side.*

History books always wait to be changed: I'm just trying to make something in this house of cards come alive.

But I'll write your name here so it doesn't go up in my smoke. I'll write it in every language that I can. In all the languages, dead and alive, and the wounded ones especially – the ones outnumbered, the ones outgunned, the ones unfit for their new century. In the tongues which you taught me, in the ones I taught myself: in the libraries, in the cold. In the orthographic shifts at the border-checks, punctuating the heart of it that does not ever change.

Samson. Shimshon. Perhaps your Hebrew name was a bud on the stem of Shimush, of 'use'. He and I both put you to good use. And I know you always felt prostituted, Samson – led and bound and used – but better that, darling, than to feel useless, believe me. All day my hands have hardly been able to write.

I can see more clearly without all the stuff that is not mine in the way. Here I am, locked in a room. The empty walls seem to have been built to remind me of myself.

What if there were two, locked in this room? A man and a woman, like you and me, like all that we were. That is all we can hope to understand from here. These little problems of the world are all we may ever turn to: for entertainment, or for grace. Think of all the problems between men and women that philosophers have yet to solve: that men are not rewarded for their kindness with any trophy of female desire, that women crying to be taken seriously is so often a funny sight, that there is always a war on somewhere that makes him say – he can't worry about all of this now, not now when there's a real fight – or else, imagine, the man being gentle, stroking her hair and telling her to remember how happy they were before all the arguments about equality ruined all their warm nights – or else, imagine, the woman asking for help, at times of pregnancy, or periods and heat, and asking at the same time every morning not to be seen as any different from him.

What happens between men and women because of all of the hoarded junk of history? And what would happen between men and women anyway? Perhaps you and I will be the first to tidy all of these accumulated things away, into two different drawers by the bed, without any argument. I suppose in a locked room, beyond all gender, and beyond all the germs put, for a test, in the petri dish, two people together would always still say, either: 'I choose you' or 'I choose the world'. It feels like that's all we were ever saying to each other, over and over. One of us had to stop it eventually.

Why do we repeat the same mistakes in our lives, over and over, like a song? Why do a whole people? Why do two people? From whence came my compulsion to ask you what your secret was? From whence came your compulsion to stick your hand inside everything that bites – right into the middle of the lion? Do we feel closest to ourselves in the never-ending arguments of every kitchen, bathroom and bed, even in the line 'we can't have this argument again', isn't there something of our deepest self, which we cannot be severed from, any more than from our heart?

Sometimes I think: give them another two thousand years, and see if they do any better. Maybe they will reach some kind of agreement, or, rather, reach some new way of agreeing. Give them as long of being equal as they have had of warring, give women as long of being free as they have had of being trampled, and then see whether it is an invented thing for you to be the one who's always made to run out and buy the croissants. In the meantime, put it off: put the war off, put the peace talks off, both of you, shut up, go outside and try to have a nice breakfast. Two thousand years. Is it long enough? They seem to find so many ways to throw the time away. They haven't improved sex very much, in all the time they have had to be getting on with things. Not compared to how much cooking has changed. You would think there'd be the same fashions, and progressions, in the other thing that people do, for pleasure, and out of need.

Perhaps between the two of us, Samson, if we dance together long enough, will figure out all of the steps and then can teach them to everyone else. Perhaps every couple tells each other that. Perhaps two people in a marriage experience every emotion felt between every man and woman who ever lived before them. That is it a lonely voyage up into the universal sigh, or else is like the little cases, brought to courts, that turn into the Law.

That is how we did not fail, perhaps. There is so much ground to map in this dark land, that all experiments fail – and so do all marriages. The monkeys sent up in the balloons are all lost, and with no scientist even monitoring their flight to begin with. We all provide equally valuable data of how we are failing God.

We can do this, Samson, if we're strong enough.

And both of us want to be strong.

I think I want to be strong. For a long time when I was a girl, and lonely, I thought it would be better to be weak than powerful, and I'd spend my summers not fighting the current of the stream that ran by my house. If I was weak, I would never be asked to choose, in a matter that could strip someone of their power. It is because I know I'm not too clever. It is for the same reason that I'll never be a mother.

But I do want to be strong.

I want to feel the strangeness of outward strength from the soft inside of the figure: the sacred lion filled with honey. I want to police the world, and I want to hate myself for doing it. I want to feel all the guilt and the sorrow of the strong for their blunt weaknesses; I will not flinch from the mirrors that the trampled will one day hold in our faces, to turn us into clay. I want to make the difficult decisions the strong make, and feel grave and feel my jaw clench. I want know what it feels like to become a man.

When the angels sing the song of those who have their own strength, they carry the banners of the red and white flags together, and they mix the colours of the procession in a conference room or on a cloud. The angels care for the strong as much for the needy. They sing the song of the strong with their quiet dignity:

And if I have been unkind
*to your snowing places of peace:*
to your Geneva
*to your Canada*
with your factual flags
*with your questioning lakes,*
If I have made dirty jokes
*at your treaties and entreaties*
at your German-efficient French,
*It was only because I knew*
that you knew
*that my refugees were bogus,*
that I did not have the requisite documents
*and all my white papers were burnt.*
That if you let me build a home in your snow
*a soft red would soon seep to the borders.*

*Wait up for me tonight, Samson. Listen out for the knock on the wall. I must be stronger than I thought I was: I think that I have found the border that I will have to cross.*

*I will push my way to you, through all of the walls of the library. After all, they're only made of paper. And I will not flinch from bringing down a building if it means we will be together. My faith commands me to destroy.*

# KOPH
'I prevented the dawning of the morning
and I cried: I hoped in thy word'

And so it was that David, just showered, was coming down
the stairs to the library room and was holding the book of
love poetry, religious poetry, mindlessly – the one that
Marie used to read out loud in their bedroom, her browned
legs resting up against the wall, in her black dress with the
stripes on the sides, and her shining hair lazing on the sandy
bed-sheets.

Then there was knocking on the door, and there was
language, making its way up the building slowly and unsure
as vines. David wouldn't answer the door in his towel,
because Ricardo had long since instructed him against this:
he was obedient even now. As he looked for his clothes in
his bedroom, he heard the front door-frame breaking – a
strangely wet sound, like fruit being thrown to the floor. He
leant against the bedroom door that he'd never sanded
down, pressing his ear on to the unwelcoming wood. There

were many voices – male voices – and David understood what was happening. He and Marie used to joke about their perfect hostage situation: maybe they'd hold a gun to his head and force him to read French philosophy books.

But they were taking a long time coming, and their language too took its time, skipping up the stairs, and wandering out of the windows. The word-noises didn't mean anything. David listened to the men and their voices pulling down the shelves of the library, opening the door to the sick-smelling basement, and all the books crunching like leaves or bones underfoot. They were so long in coming to get him, that David opened his bedroom door. He walked down the steps, one hand on his towel, one hand on the railing, slow like an entrance at an Oscar ceremony, golden as an Oscar, an alpha award.

He saw twelve men in dark clothes, and guns in a treacle-textured black of oil and ink. They began to shout at him, their mouths opening up like wounds. David understood what was happening. But he didn't understand the words. Was it even Arabic? Was it not Farsi? All his languages failed him now; his tongue became as a flat tombstone upon the bottom of his mouth. He shook his head as they shouted at him. Three of the men drew their guns at the same instant, choreographed, like ballet.

The first shot made David step back, and the next two made him step forward, and all the other shots snapped him into a shudder, as his towel fell. And so it was that David danced, as the morning sun came through the window: the way that boys and men dance without the aid of women, both light and limb-filled. Just as Maimonades wrote of Samson: like a bell that strikes first this way and then that. But unlike Samson, David understood.

\*

In the months after Marie had left, David had grown used to knocking on the library door, and he rose to them, at any hour. The soft rattling of the door-frame, or an even tapping on the downstairs windows, had replaced the internationals' parties and the happy torture of Marie's whole-universe of presence. He'd learnt to hear the gentle knocking above the sound of wind or gunfire or protests. It was the main thing he got up for now: for Sara.

Sara was the name, one of the many names, that Marie had never learnt: it was the girl who'd found the pornography the volunteers had left in her house. After Marie had left for enemy territory, David didn't open the library for three days. Noises would fly out of the building, the noises of a strong man who has found himself suddenly blinded. These were what made Sara knock on the door. The other girls would remain too shy of him. But he'd seen her when she was broken down, the screaming girl in her bedroom of pink bears: now she was rebuilt and ready for honesty.

'Hello. I'm sorry to hear . . .'

David rubbed his stubble and squinted through his just-woken haze.

'Oh. Hi. It's . . .'

'I'm Sara.' She didn't seem to mind he didn't remember. 'I'm sorry about Anne-Marie.' She looked sorry the way adults want to look sorry: she had perfected, or simply felt, the tight-rope tone of frank and brave kindnesses. 'I thought you might like someone to help you.'

'Well, um. That's very kind, but . . .' David looked around, as if confused that it was morning, that he was here, that he was David. He could taste at least that he hadn't brushed his teeth.

'I think you need someone to help you. Why don't you have a shower. Then you can tell me what needs doing in the library.'

She was tall, for a thirteen-year-old, and her eyes were wide and intelligent. And so she became his second-in-command at the library, which felt strange for David only because Marie had never really helped him running the building anyway. They ordered new books, created a system of cataloguing them, and cut an old book of maps up to informatively decorate the walls. David asked her what sorts of books she thought people here would like to read.

'All sorts of books. For all sorts of people.'

'Oh. Sorry, Sara.' But she laughed.

At times it was hard for David to navigate, the difficulty of being loved inappropriately: she was a girl, he was a grown man, and he could tell, though it shamed him to admit it, that she was in love with him. There was no textbook for how to deal with this. He wished he could dream up some thirteen-year-old boy to hold her so she wouldn't look at him like that. He wondered if among the death-count of the children here, there was a boy, tall for a thirteen-year-old, with intelligent eyes, who'd been invented and intended for Sara. He was, he knew, frightened of becoming a professor, of moulding a girl, wracking her with the diseases of his imperfect thinking, then sending her out to do the dirty work of the world. He tried to listen more than talk: he hoped to show her that there was at least one adult who took her seriously. A thirteen-year-old needs to be taken seriously.

So he'd teach her, but more importantly, she'd teach him. She asked what England was like, what being Jewish was like, what university was like. She'd come to him with a book she'd pulled from the shelves, with a question and itching for answers, or with arguments and a head-full of answers of her own. The noises and worries outside seemed to grow smaller for both of them, as they talked about their favourite stories, their favourite leaders, their ideal worlds and how confusing people were.

Still sometimes he grew too dark for talking, so Sara would send him letters. She'd push them under the door when she knew she shouldn't knock today, because he was pacing around inside, or drinking up on the roof in the daytime, or staring angrily at himself in the mirror – she knew or felt he did these things: thirteen-year-olds should be taken seriously. Before her breakdown, the letters she'd pushed under the library door were just nothings, girl-things, luridly covered in rainbows, and stickers of pandas that her pen-pal in Holland had sent her. But now they were arguments about why it was important to be kind to the elderly, a description of how foolish her father looked when he fell asleep after dinner, a written dream of all the things she'd do if Palestine was free. She didn't mind he never wrote back or mentioned them. She was on the other side of something now, and was unselfconscious about how happy he made her.

She wrote the letter that came under the door that day, which David had found just before washing. It was like the only piece of paper left in the world: he ran to the bath to prepare himself for what he knew was to come.

# RESH

'I beheld the transgressors, and was grieved'

Mohammad had sent the message to David through the children because they were the only ones who could carry it. As soon as Marie had run from the house, Mohammad contacted Amnesty International. He had no other numbers, David had never told him his, and he hadn't wanted to be the one to ask. He called the Amnesty office in London. But the man he wanted to talk to was in New York. They transferred him: Mohammad had met him when he worked in Geneva, and knew that his wife worked on a project in the West Bank.

'Tell her to tell the children in her village to tell the children in David's village.' Mohammad found out on the Internet that they were only three miles apart. And to think that it had come to relying on the peace-keepers and the human rights lawyers; that it had come to really needing them, at a time like this. It was unexpected as the return of religion that had come to knock on all their teenage doors.

And so it was that he passed on the only message that he knew would be delivered, the only fact that would deliver David back. It said: 'Marie is coming back to you.'

\*

Where to begin again? Perhaps by going backwards:

Twenty-five years later, Mohammad would be teaching at Oxford. He would pay off the mortgage on his house with the money from his textbook on new developments in international relations. He'd spend most of his evenings in a quiet restaurant in North Parade, the little street that was permanently done up like a Blitz-era fete. He would be better at marking than at lectures. He would never buy a car.

In the next few years after the moment, which saw him past the end of their century's first decade, Mohammad would live in New York, in Washington DC and in London. He'd spend a weekend in Montreal talking to a woman he had met at a conference over five cups of English tea and two French croissants. Other than that he would be by himself. His hair would change imperceptibly. He'd go through six coats and three apartments. He would spend many hours on an aeroplane, offering up his aisle seat, or window seat, or any seat, and awkwardly trying to open the tin foil top of the orange juice without squirting it into the lap of the person sitting next to him. He'd learn four underground systems by heart, and learnt to adapt to the changes on London's tube when he went back there. He became the only man in London who helped girls and women, with their suitcases and children's prams, on the slippery underground steps. He diligently learnt all the facts of each new war and ethnic conflict.

In the next few weeks after the moment, Mohammad would print off all of his documents, just in case his computer and disks were somehow damaged in the transit to America. He re-read a lot of what he printed off. He had written so much that he had forgotten about. He started to pack up his law books, and realised that many of them were already out of date. This was how he learnt that Israel doesn't have Oxfam shops, and he had to put them in the bin, which he didn't mind so much, except it was bad for the environment. Waiting for his new job to be finalised, and with most of his things already in boxes, he began to frequent one of the tatty blue-and-dirt coloured cafes by the beach, and one day would be accosted by a pervert on a quiet stretch of the shore. Back at the apartment, he would have some trouble making the plastic labels stick on to his boxes. He would have some trouble with the contract for the apartment. He would have some trouble at the airport.

In those next few hours in his house after the moment, after hearing the news, he put his arms around his first pillow. This was to be an act of many years' worth of Sundays. Marie had never told him that this was how she'd spent her childhood: he did not know to what great ranks he had enrolled now. It took him over ten minutes of holding to make the pillow-cover feel like the shape of a body. It took him longer to cry. He stroked his own head for the first time, in those waiting hours, pretending that the hand was somebody else's. He checked the BBC news website seven times. He read a story about a fluke hurricane in Yorkshire, and clicked on the Sports section without even noticing. He put a pan of water on the stove, and it boiled itself into oblivion because he forgot to take it off.

In the first two minutes after he'd received the news, Mohammad rested his head in his folded arms, and rested his folded arms on the counter in his kitchen. He closed his eyes. He saw the orange and grey against the blue sky that was the default of all of their minds. He opened his eyes and saw, unfocused, the white of the counter-top from which he'd cleaned off the cake-crumbs that Anne-Marie had left earlier that week. He closed his eyes for a very long time. The phone rang and he did not answer it. It was David's mother.

In the first two seconds of the news he breathed out. He must have breathed in very hard afterwards. He didn't remember, when he thought back to that time, which in any case he tried not to.

Finally, in the heart of Mohammad, he was tired as a library. He remembered all the kisses, all the words they'd said, but he couldn't remember the events in any order. He didn't know how any of the things in their lives had happened, he didn't know how much he had been loved. But he knew how much he had loved them. He didn't think of himself, but of how alone, and like children, Anne-Marie and David must have felt in those last moments: alone and like children. That was all he thought.

He'd read somewhere among his UN reports that the average age of a Palestinian suicide-bomber is seventeen, and the age of an Israeli conscript only one year older. But he only realised with his head on the white counter that the whole war was a war of children, all alone holding pillows. He didn't know who was the most alone, in that time: Marie, without even a voice, a fixed name, or David, shouldering his troubled strength. It took Mohammad a long time to realise that only he understood how alone, and that

their different lonelinesses comforted each other, somewhere, at the same sad distance from the light. Mohammad
stroked his own hair. He held his own hand, whispered his
own name, said 'ssh, ssh, ssh,' for comfort, as if it was
someone else. It felt both strange and familiar, and so did all
of his thoughts. He tried to put his arms around his own
feeling of what it was like to be only a messenger.

# TAU

'Let my cry come near before thee'

But even her endings were false, because Mohammad saw her once more, or so he thought, unreliable as the dark-sky overhang of his eyelids and the dimmed lights of the solemn conference-room could be. It had been two years since the end of history for them, and the world for him was now one of documenting, retreating, and annotating the real that there was once. He'd begun to feel a warmth of sorts towards the plastic furniture in rooms like this. He tried to think about the world from the point of view of furniture, because to furniture you are a ridiculous thing, that comes and goes without rhythm or meaning, that might as well be dead, or will be soon. He liked to be the last one to leave a conference room, to acknowledge this fact as he turned the lights off.

His colleague Dominic brought them both coffees, plastic-cupped, as they waited for everyone else to file in and sit down. Mohammad was slowly getting to know the people he worked with – through enough late nights and early mornings, they ended up having to meet each other with barriers down too often to remain completely formal. Dominic would wake Mohammad up when he fell asleep at his desk in the office; much coffee was bought on behalf of others, and the debt repaid diligently with more coffee in turn.

'I'm not sure I can stay for the whole talk. I have to get my paper ready.'

'How's that going?' Mohammad asked as he focused on trying to take the lid off his coffee without spilling it.

'I found some new sources and had to start over completely.'

'But you're happy with it now?'

'Yeah. I reckon. It's time to let go of it anyway.'

'I know what you mean.'

'Yeah. Are you working on a paper right now?'

'Nothing in particular.'

Their conversation evaporated, settled on the windows, and they found their way to two of the eternal-chairs. The other members of the conference were loitering purposefully outside, or on the edges of the inside of the room. There were displays about Darfur in the corridors: photographs of beautiful skies, crowded camps, and burning. The organisers thought they'd begin the weekend of lectures with this seminar, 'First-Hand Testimonies From Darfur', before they got down to the real stuff, the academic discussions, of the following day's talks. Everyone respectfully feigned interest.

A man with large hands was standing behind them, talking about his work in Al Fashir. More people moved quietly into the room, and several separated from the polite crowd to move to the chairs set by the side of the platform, for the speakers. Dominic tried to talk to Mohammad about his latest research, but his eyes were focused on the two figures sitting on plastic chairs next to the podium: the engineer who was billed to talk about his work in the IDP camps, and his daughter, a young woman in a headscarf, her eyes unlined with makeup or memories that he could trace. Something had softened in her face, and the dark hair underneath her headscarf created an effect of kinds of depth. Her father spoke first, about the difficulties of being an engineer there, about the need for better-designed refugee tents. Then the young woman was invited to talk, about how war affects women in Darfur. She walked unself-consciously to the centre, and looked calmly around the room as she began.

'In the camps where I work, everyone can be divided between those who have been raped and those who haven't. It's very often the most meaningful way to divide people. And in the division of those who have, are nearly all of the women I've met there. Nine-year-old girls who were raped by groups of armed men. Women who were raped when they were pregnant. Women who were raped in front of their families. They were either left to bleed outside, or abducted and forced into sex slavery for the militias. They were called godless and they were called whores. Almost all of the women I have met there.'

Mohammad had always had a rare ability to be moved by facts, and make his home in them. Every statement: 180,000 Sudanese dead; 1.2 million displaced – he could be touched by these things like love-letters and smiles, as much as he was still touched by smiles, both David's and Marie's. And if he hardly spoke it was because it was too much for him to convey how everything touched him. His infinite feeling extended to the engineer's daughter talking on the platform: he hoped she wasn't nervous to talk, but her voice maintained a deliberate yet unlaboured slowness, a perfect pace that she must have developed somewhere else.

'I don't know what to say about the fact that the militias like to sing songs about rape. I don't know what to say about the fact they cut open stomachs of pregnant women, to pull out what they consider to be an enemy child. Perhaps it's wrong to mention that the people they do it to are also Muslims, as though that makes it worse, when it is already the worst thing. But it is one of the many things that makes this war so bitter and so hard to understand. And when I say that the government stands by, I don't just mean in the way that I stand by, which I do, being privileged and able to leave. I mean they stand by in the sense of watching and participating in these acts.'

Mohammad was distracted for a moment as Dominic took out his notebook, which people rarely did at these informal speeches. Everyone in the room listened politely, with appropriate solemnity, for the subject matter, but also for the figure that the young woman took on the stand. There was no blondeness and no spark, and this person was a better person, they all knew, because she didn't smile so much. Mohammad didn't catch her name, but it didn't matter, because it wasn't Marie's – Anne-Marie's, Annie's – name any more anyway: she had ninety-nine and none when he thought of her, which he tried not to do.

Three more people rose in turn to talk after she'd sat down next to her father. She sat without moving, but without effort in her stillness. A Sudanese woman who was working in the south explained the difficulties of combating female genital mutilation during a war. A German man took the audience through the difficulties that charity workers have in applying for visas, how this was harming relief efforts, and what could be done about it. Mohammad listened entirely, attentively, making notes, forming questions to ask, all the while half-paralysed by the presence of the girl he'd known and her father.

Afterwards, the dark-haired girl left with the tall engineer, similar to her, sad-eyed but still practical-looking. He was the same height and age as the professor, but it was the opposite story, it was clear: from how she carried herself, from the evenness of her voice – she belonged to herself now that she worked for other people, she was no longer merely awash in other people's times and minds.

This was the best he could've hoped for, prayed for, as he pointlessly had, so many nights in those times after the end: that she, or a future-she, of a new consistency, had found a way back into the world, a way of interacting with the imperfection of people, which had once seemed to overpower her.

And yet now, ashamed of it, Mohammad felt sadness, the utter sadness of beyond-sadness, that comes when you no longer have anything to pray for: the sadness of a God dying, like Valhalla melting in the sky. He was the first to leave the conference-room this time, and stood up against the wall outside, beyond-sad and his mind all empty of everything. It was too sad to think about: how he could be sad that she'd changed, and had found a purpose.

Because it is a hard thing to do, to praise those who don't try to understand, emphasise and make connections, hard to admit that, at certain moments, their alpha-smiles and beauties are a substitute enough for caring. But he knew a little better now: that when you start, when you even try to start to try, to try to care and to change things, that the connection is so hard, cracking, so easily broken – that in an adult world of guesses and solutions, it makes sense to dream of that perfect place, which exists before you mix yourself with world; before you choose, make a commitment, and, with all the best intentions, get it completely wrong. He understood now: this perfect place, these perfect people, of arrogance and lightness, of too-loud laughing and disdain, existed but to come to you, not arrogantly but in humility, in their veils or in their vividness, to remind you sitting there, in every conference room, in every shiny, Sheikh-endowed library, in every book, in every report and reported experience, come back to tell you that, after all attempts, this still is not your truth and it never will be.

## Acknowledgements

I would like to thank Maggie Hamand, Jane Havell and everyone at The Maia Press for all their hard work and patience in putting this book together. Thank you to everyone at the Canadian Rhodes Foundation for the opportunity to study Arabic and finish my book in Montreal. My friends had to put up with even more than usual while I was writing this, and all deserve big drinks and cake: Loic Menzies – for reading the first draft, getting me through everything, and for letting me steal your one-liners . . . let's get married. (I'm kidding.) Thank you to my best friends Sara Charrot and Franziska von Blumenthal – for too much to mention. Thank you to Jim Grant for all our talks, and for your patience. Thank you to Jess Charrot for Christmas, kindness and putting up with my jokes. Thank you to Himanshu Ojha for memorising every line of *The West Wing* with me, and thank you to Jordan Rowell for your music collection. Thank you to Tom Skelton for the tree-climbing, getting me through finals, and for your steadfast belief in a railway tunnel underneath the Atlantic Ocean. I believe you. Thank you to my wonderful McRobies – Dad, Fiona, Ellen, Helen and Charlie – for everything.